Michael's lips found hers, but this time tenderness merged with passion, and they moved with a single intent toward the couch. He lowered Karen gently, pressing her against him so that their bodies seemed to mold, to fuse, and Karen responded to Michael with an instinctive arching, wanting him as she had never wanted anyone before.

His hands explored her, those wonderful fingers setting forth on a quest so evocative that she felt herself filled with a soaring rapture that was sweeter than music. Gradually Karen found herself impelled to touch him as he was touching her, and with slow deliberation she unbuttoned his shirt, pressing her lips to his chest.

At that moment Michael paused, and Karen could see that he was making a visible attempt to get control of himself.

"Don't stop," she breathed with an invasive intimacy that carried with it its own brand of fire....

Dear Reader,

It is our pleasure to bring you romance novels that go beyond category writing. The settings of **Harlequin American Romance** give a sense of place and culture that is uniquely American, and the characters are warm and believable. The stories are of "today" and have been chosen to give variety within the vast scope of romance fiction.

Meg Hudson creates an eerie paradise in a wooded, isolated compound in Vermont. Karen Morse and Michael Stanhope are lovers who must overcome their separate pasts. The touch of mystery in this love story will hold you spellbound until its conclusion.

From the early days of Harlequin, our primary concern has been to bring you novels of the highest quality. **Harlequin American Romance** is no exception. Enjoy!

Vivian Stephens

Vivian Stephens
Editorial Director
Harlequin American Romance
919 Third Avenue,
New York, N.Y. 10022

To Love
a Stranger

MEG HUDSON

Harlequin Books

TORONTO • NEW YORK • LONDON
AMSTERDAM • PARIS • SYDNEY • HAMBURG
STOCKHOLM • ATHENS • TOKYO • MILAN

With family memories, especially
of Lucy and Fred

Published October 1983

First printing August 1983

ISBN 0-373-16025-9

Printed in Canada

Chapter One

The dream came in those supposedly darkest hours before dawn. It began, as it always did, with a blazing sky so intense that it dazzled her; even in sleep she thrust her arm up, guarding her eyes against the sunbursts of gold, piercing shafts of light that penetrated the endless expanse of blue. She turned away from the plane's windshield, shutting them out, and saw that Keith, beside her in the cockpit, was smiling. But it was an odd smile.

She started to speak to him, and then the world ended. Or, at the least, it turned upside down, and they seemed to spiral toward eternity, the plane seeking, reaching, finding, in a terrible, terminal moment.

She awoke, drenched, sitting up in bed, groping for the lamp on the table by her side. Light spilled across the pale green, rumpled sheets, but no warmth came with the light, no solace.

They should have buried me with him, she thought. Keith Morse and Karen Morse, side by side. R.I.P.

She got up and fumbled for her robe, then slipped it on, knotted it loosely. Her arm ached, this too a constant reminder, and she flexed fingers that still failed sometimes to respond to her bidding. She went out into the tiny kitchenette and made herself a cup of hot milk and then sat at the living room window, sipping it, waiting and watching until dawn crept over Manhattan. Then, in the near daylight, she went back to bed and slept fitfully until the alarm rang at seven.

As she dressed, facing her pallid reflection in the full-length closet mirror, Karen knew that Hugh would realize the moment he saw her that she'd had the dream again. Hugh was a doctor, which made it very difficult to keep things from him. He was also in love with her, which made him that much more perceptive. This was a problem, because it was not a love she returned, not in the same way, although she would be grateful to him forever. But he, fortunately, did not push it, although he told her, wryly, that he still had hopes she would wake up someday to discover that she was working for Prince Charming in a white coat. In the meantime, he let her set their pace, for Hugh, bless him, had no wish to make her suffer any more than she already had suffered. And he was married. Unhappily married, but married nevertheless.

She smiled faintly at her reflection, soundlessly accused herself of trying out for a martyr role, then gave her naturally wavy ash-blond hair an added flick of the brush. There were shadows beneath the wide clear amber eyes that made her coloring so unusual, but it would take more than a makeup stick to camouflage them today, she knew, so she opted for a bit more lipstick and let it go at that.

Karen walked to work that morning. June was a

good month in New York, and that early in the day there was a surprising freshness to the city air. She cut across town to Madison Avenue, headed north, and then turned down a sidestreet toward Fifth Avenue, stopping midway along the block at the discreet, converted town house where Hugh had his office.

Trudy Richardson had arrived ahead of her and had already donned her white uniform and adjusted her absurd little frilled nurse's cap with the broad black band.

"Hi," she greeted Karen. "The coffee just finished perking."

"I'll take a cup," Karen said promptly. "I need something to wake me up."

She settled in at her desk in the reception area, noting regretfully that the pink peony an elderly patient had brought her yesterday from a New Jersey garden was beginning to shed its petals and would have to go. She cast her eye over the appointment schedule. It promised to be a full day and it would be starting early, as Hugh was not operating this morning. There were several letters to be written, but she was sure she could sandwich them in as the day progressed. There were phone calls to be made, but she'd sandwich them in too. She was amused at her newfound efficiency.

She heard a door close and could feel Hugh's eyes upon her even before she looked up. They were grave, behind his gold-rimmed glasses. He said, "Again?"

She nodded.

"Karen," he began, "I'm an orthopedic surgeon, not a psychiatrist. But it stands to reason that you've got to do something about this. It's draining you."

"Are you suggesting a shrink again?" she asked, trying to force a smile.

He shook his head. "Not necessarily, though the fact that you tried one psychiatrist and didn't hit it off with him doesn't prove that it was the wrong course. It's just that it's been nearly two years—"

"Less seven days," she interrupted and avoided his eyes.

"You shouldn't still be counting them," he told her grimly.

She could hear Trudy in the examining room. There was the sound of instruments clattering and a window blind being snapped up. She asked dully, "What would you suggest?"

"Involvement," Hugh told her briefly. "Involvement with something, or someone, sufficiently intriguing to *matter* to you. I might add that I know precisely what I'm doing to my own cause by telling you that!"

Now their eyes did meet. His were frankly unhappy. What a fool his wife was, Karen thought. If she tried to meet him halfway . . . .

But the chances of this, she knew, were slim. She had met Sara only occasionally, on drop-in visits to the office. But even slight exposure had shown her that Sara was primarily interested in only one thing, one person. Herself.

Maybe when you get down to it most of us need shrinks, Karen thought, and the thought caused an involuntary smile.

"What's funny?" Dr. Hugh MacKnight asked her.

"Nothing, really," she told him. Which unfortunately was true.

She was glad to be reprieved by a phone call from a colleague who wanted to discuss a case into which Hugh had been called on consultation.

Involvement. The word lingered, coming back into her mind at odd moments during this busier-than-usual day. Involvement with something or someone in an area where it would matter. That, she warned herself, could mean getting in deep, and she was not at all sure she wanted to get in deep with anything or anyone. She had traveled that route.

With the workday at an end Trudy, who was divorced, suggested supper and an early movie, but Karen refused, pleading a fictitious engagement, and suspected that Trudy knew her for the fraud she was. Hugh paused to ask if she'd stop by with him for a drink at the Carlyle before she went home, but again she refused, for the purely selfish reason that she definitely didn't want to get involved with Hugh of all people. She sensed intuitively that to do so in her present state would be preamble to ruining a friendship that was very precious to her.

She was left to close up the office, locking the door behind her and walking out into a nearly perfect early summer evening, with no place to go but home and nothing to go home to, and no idea at all of how soon this situation was to change, nor how radically.

It was nearly ten o'clock when Maida phoned. Karen, who had been trying but failing to become interested in a movie on TV, was glad to be diverted by her favorite cousin, but early on in their conversation she began to get the distinct impression that this was not a casual call.

This was confirmed when Maida asked, her voice anxious, "Are you permitted to drive yet?"

"I don't know," Karen admitted. "There's been no occasion to ask Hugh about it. I no longer have a car, anyway. When you live in New York, a car can be more of a liability than an asset."

"Oh," Maida said, and there was acute disappointment in the single word.

"Is there some reason why I *should* have a car?" Karen asked, exploring.

"It's the easiest way to get here."

"To Boston?"

"I'm not in Boston," her cousin told her. "I'm in Vermont."

"Vermont?"

"Grand Isle. I'm at Jerry's father's place."

"Is Jerry on vacation?"

There was a definite moment of hesitation, then Maida said, "No, Jerry is in Boston."

"Then is Jerry's father with you?"

Again, there was a pause, then Maida said, "No, he's still at the embassy in London. He'll be there through this next summer, at least. Since Chad died he doesn't seem to have any desire to come back to the States. Karen...."

"Yes?"

"I'm alone here and I'm miserable." There was desperation in Maida's voice. "Please," she continued, "you've got to come up!"

"Maida, I couldn't possibly!"

"You could! It isn't that far. You can drive to Plattsburgh and take the ferry across Lake Champlain, or you can take the Interstate to Burlington and then switch off onto Route Two, and it's just a few miles farther along.''

Karen frowned. ''I have a job,'' she hedged.

''You said yourself it's mostly therapy,'' Maida reminded her.

''It was, in the beginning, but I've worked into it.''

''Will you at least ask Dr. MacKnight for a brief leave of absence?'' Maida's voice was muffled, and Karen suspected that her usually sophisticated cousin was crying. She said, sniffing, ''I wouldn't be begging if I didn't need you!''

Caution had become instinctive these past two years. Karen said slowly, ''I'll speak to Hugh tomorrow.''

''Couldn't you call him tonight? I'm *frightened*, Karen.''

Maida's urgency communicated across the wires. ''Is it that bad?'' Karen found herself asking.

''Yes!''

The decision was made. ''All right,'' she said. ''As soon as I've spoken to Hugh I'll call you back.''

Once she had hung up the phone, however, she didn't immediately return to it, and when finally she started to dial Hugh's number she did so with reluctant fingers. As his phone began to ring, she told herself that she should have asked Maida more questions before going this far.

She disliked calling Hugh at home. She had done so only once before, this when she awoke with a bad sore throat one morning and knew that she couldn't make it in to work. Sara had answered the phone, and Karen had been quite sure that she had awakened her. A few days later Sara had stopped in at the office on one of her rare visits, her cool blue eyes lingering appraisingly on Karen, though there was no reason, no reason at all, why a single, bona fide phone call should have aroused any suspicion. Despite her strong, personal affection for Hugh, despite the bond that had been forged between them these past two years as he worked over her badly injured arm in the effort to make it whole and functional again, she had no wish to become involved in a triangle.

So now she dialed reluctantly, and as luck would have it Sara answered, and Sara had been drinking. She was overly polite, and there was a decided edge to her voice as she called her husband to the phone. It came to Karen that it might not be such a bad idea to go up to Vermont for a few days. It was only recently that Hugh had come to the point of asking her to stop by for a drink with him after work. Once or twice she had yielded, and it had been pleasant. Too pleasant. Hugh was charming, and he was hungry for the very kind of companionship that she could give him. In a sense, he was a man drowning; his marriage was on the rocks, he was reaching out for someone, something. She knew the feeling. Her own marriage had been on the rocks in those months just before the plane crash.

Hugh said, "Karen?"

"Yes."

She told him briefly about Maida's call, and he said, "What is it, do you think?"

Karen laughed. "Maida's an actress. At least she was, and quite a good one too before she married Gerald Stanhope. Probably she's imagining banshees, something like that. Though why she should be up there in the first place—"

"I think," said Hugh, "that you'd better go find out."

She sensed his reluctance, for small as such a trip might be in the overall scheme of things it was, nevertheless, rather like cutting an umbilical cord. In many ways she had been tied to him these past two years, more dependent upon him than she had realized. This was a step toward independence. As a doctor, she knew, he wanted her to take it. But as a man. . . .

She said, not quite ready to let go, "We can talk about it tomorrow."

"No," he said. "I'm operating all morning, and I have a light office schedule in the afternoon. There's no need for you to come in. Trudy and I will manage."

"Very well, then," she said, feeling a bit rebuffed because he could dispense with her services so easily, "tomorrow is Wednesday. I'll go up to Vermont, but I'll only plan to stay till the weekend. You can expect me back in the office bright and early Monday morning."

"I wonder," Hugh said, an odd note in his voice.

"What is there to wonder about?"

"I don't know," he said, and tried to laugh, but it was a poor attempt. "Who's to tell what you'll find up there in Vermont?"

Chapter Two

The rental car, a blue compact not unlike the one she'd had before the plane crash, was waiting for Karen at the airport in Burlington.

She slid into the driver's seat, her fingers tentatively touching the steering wheel. It was an odd feeling, and now she wished she'd had a chance to practice driving again before setting out in strange territory, although Hugh had told her it should pose no problem. He had, however, advised flying to the nearest airport and renting a car there, rather than attempting a drive of over three hundred miles entirely on her own.

"But you'll be all right," he had assured her on the phone, and she had wanted to cry out, Don't be so sure!

She shifted into drive and cautiously pressed the accelerator, glad that the airport parking lot was almost empty so that she had room in which to experiment before she took to the road.

She had, in fact, been panicking at the thought of going forth on her own, she was beginning to think that she should find herself another shrink, but then

Hugh said, "Give me a call and let me know how it's going. And don't worry about the job."

Now, almost immediately, she realized that Hugh had been right. The responses were there, just as he had said they would be, and her left hand compensated for the strength her right hand lacked. Also, typing in his office had brought back a certain tone and accompanying dexterity to her fingers.

She glanced at her watch. It was nearly two. She had skipped breakfast this morning, and for the first time in a long while she really felt hungry. She swung out of the parking lot and, once on the road, looked for a drive-in restaurant, and was soon rewarded.

She ordered a cheeseburger, French fries—something she never succumbed to, ordinarily—and a strawberry milk shake, took the food back out to the car, and, feeling almost in a holiday mood, switched on the radio. They were playing "Light My Fire", and when she heard the words, they brought back a flood of memories.

Karen found herself clenching her fists, making her arm ache in the process, her eyes burning with all the tears she had never shed.

Keith *had* been untrue. Like the words of the song that was something she was going to have to face up to, that and quite a few other things. She would, in time, have to be able to listen to Debussy or to a Beethoven sonata for the piano, without feeling as if she were being torn apart, without the terrible, personal grief of knowing that her own fingers would never again move over the keys as they once had, all that was in her to give flowing out in interpretation and perfect technical mastery.

Hugh MacKnight had said, "You'll play again." He had refrained from saying, "You'll play concerts again."

The song ended, and she turned the volume low before the next piece began, forcing herself to go on eating her lunch, but the fun, the savor, were gone.

Keith. She let herself think of him and inevitably the thought became an ache as she remembered the first time she had ever met him, six summers ago. She had played with the Boston Pops that year. She was only twenty, and the critics had prophesied great things for her.

The Sunday after the concert she had gone down to Cape Cod with friends. There was a clambake on the beach; she could remember gasping with delight when the tarpaulin cover was thrown back, and she smelled the wonderful, salt-tinged aroma and saw the lobsters, gleaming coral on their seaweed beds.

A voice at her side said, "Quite a sight, isn't it?" and she turned to face a tall man with pleasant features, a lazy smile, and light, amused blue eyes. Her heart constricted—at least, people always said it was one's heart. Whatever, it was a tight, tugging feeling.

"You're Karen Kent, aren't you?"

She nodded, and he said, "I'm Keith Morse. I was one of the people enchanted by you at the Pops concert the other night."

She had smiled at this, then later followed his lead as he initiated her into clambake etiquette. The steamer clams, he explained, were to be eaten first, and washed down with broth. Next came the lobster, accompanied by succulent corn on the cob, sausages, and both white and sweet potatoes. All of these things were part of the "bake," which had steamed for hours over hot rocks, seaweed-covered, tarpaulin-topped, so that they emerged with an indescribable flavor perfectly in keeping with the setting and a night made magic by a huge disc of a moon rising over lace-edged water.

Keith, who, like herself, made New York his home base, asked her to dinner the following week, and they soon became a pair. When Karen went on concert tour the following fall she missed him terribly, and when he flew to Chicago two weeks before Christmas she literally fell into his arms and agreed when he asked her to marry him.

After a simple civil ceremony they went back to New York for Christmas at the Beekman Place apartment where his father and his stepmother lived. They were both pleasant enough to her—they were inherently polite people—yet there was a rather aloof coldness to their manner that made her doubt if she could ever really like either of them.

For that matter, the new year was not very far along before she began to realize that she wasn't at all sure she *liked* Keith. Romance was one thing—passion, she conceded, might be a better word. Affection, respect, liking, *love,* were, she knew now, something else entirely.

Keith worked in his father's publishing firm, and his job involved a good deal of traveling. Because of her own concert schedule plus television appearances, interviews, and all the other facets of her life as an artist, she and Keith were apart much of the time. As time passed, the years merging, she began to give thought to relinquishing her career so that she could devote herself to being his wife, yet she knew that her fame was very important to Keith, in fact she began to suspect that it was the most important thing about her, to him. For instance, he relished coming backstage after a concert to claim her as his property in front of everyone.

Finally rumors began to filter back to her, which she at first tried to ignore because it was too painful to think that there were other women in Keith's life. The clues became increasingly obvious, however. There were phone calls sometimes at the apartment they shared in New York's East Sixties, and there were letters from some of the cities he visited in the course of his work that certainly were not from business contacts!

Karen found herself being deliberately blind to most of this because Keith was her husband, and she was old-fashioned in her ideas about marriage. Although she had lost her parents within a short space of time when she was in her teens, she had seen the best of marriage in their relationship to each other during her formative years. Marriage, in her opinion, was worth a total effort, and she was prepared to give it.

Two years ago she and Keith had gone back to Cape Cod on a kind of nostalgia trip. This had been his suggestion, and she had agreed to it eagerly, sure that it would make a turning point for the best in their faltering relationship.

Keith rented a plane at LaGuardia in which to make the trip. He was an experienced pilot and lately had been talking about buying a plane, provided his father would agree to a loan. Although Karen disliked the thought of being obligated to her father-in-law, she was in favor of the idea. A plane of their own would open up weekend prospects for just the two of them. She could learn to fly; in fact Keith had an instructor's license and so could teach her. She told herself that it would mean the beginning of a whole new life.

The June afternoon they flew into Hyannis had near perfect weather. Keith had reserved rooms at a popular resort complex, and while the place was attractive, Karen was somewhat disappointed by this. She would have preferred something less modern in a more secluded part of the Cape.

Keith, however, was in a convivial mood. He called friends, who promptly joined them for a late dinner, and to Karen's dismay, he drank too much.

He was not at his best the next morning and had a bloody Mary with brunch, which disturbed her. She had heard enough pilot conversation between Keith and his friends to know that even the dregs of liquor in one's system did not mix with flying. Nevertheless, when he hoisted his glass, grinned, and said, "This'll fix me up," she had believed him.

On the way to the airport she spoke to him about taking flying lessons. He was pleased, if not quite as enthusiastic as she might have thought he would be, and for once he sensed her disappointment.

"Honey," he said apologetically, "I'm not quite up to things this morning."

"Maybe you should have slept longer," she suggested.

Keith shook his head. "No, I'll be all right."

Still, he was silent for the remainder of the ride, and Karen sensed a tenseness in him as he went through the usual inspection check with the plane.

But he smiled reassuringly across at her as he prepared to take off, and it seemed to her that he was handling the controls just as capably as he always did.

It was a beautiful day, the sky was larkspur blue and cloudless. Karen had never understood just what happened, just what went wrong. Pilot error, they said later, after the federal authorities had completed their investigation, and that, of course, was precisely what it had been. Alcohol and flying didn't mix. Keith had proved that conclusively.

Now, sitting at the wheel of her rented car, she shuddered. She found, to her surprise, that she had finished the cheeseburger, the milk shake, and most of the French fries, while lost in her somber reflections. Now she tossed the empty containers into a trash can, then started forth again.

Outside of Burlington she struck off on Route Two, first heading north, then veering to the west, over the low sandbar bridge that connected the Vermont mainland with the Lake Champlain Islands.

Champlain itself, named for the famous French explorer who long ago had discovered it, spread out before her, a vast inland sea that was today a breathtaking deep sapphire in color. The western skyline was punctuated by the jagged peaks of New York State's Adirondack Mountains, while Vermont's own Green Mountains filled the sky to the north and east with their own verdant magnificence.

This was incredibly beautiful country, Karen found herself thinking, though Route Two, itself, was a rather nondescript road, traversing terrain that was still sparsely settled for the most part. Old-fashioned motor courts with cabins were more the rule here than starkly modern motels. Campgrounds and trailer parks were interspersed with farms whose fields must run clear down to the lake in many places. There were numerous summer camps, and intriguing dirt side roads that would be fun to explore if one had time to wander. In all, though, it was as if the highway were merely a transition point from one place to another, and in a sense it was exactly that, a link between Burlington and Montreal.

It was difficult to differentiate between South Hero and Grand Isle, but in her directions Maida had described first a gas station and then a general store, and as she passed them both Karen began to get her bearings. If Maida was accurate, the Stanhopes' driveway should be about another quarter mile on the left, and it was. Karen saw the white name sign lettered with black that Maida had told her about and she turned onto a narrow, rutty dirt road, then quickly reduced her speed to a minimum, for it not only was potholed but began, almost immediately, to weave around in a series of curves.

She drove cautiously, wondering what one could possibly hope to do if another car suddenly loomed up ahead. There was no place in which to turn off, in fact there was a gully on her side of the road that, while not really deep, was deep enough to be dangerous.

Finally she rounded a bend and came to a dividing point. The road forked, each segment leading toward the lakefront. There were no further signs, nothing for guidance, and Karen stopped, perplexed, for Maida had said nothing about this.

Well, left or right, it was a matter of choice, and she opted for the right fork first. It curved through a forest of magnificent firs and slender silver birches, then rounding a bend, she saw a house ahead and drew in her breath with delight.

Maida, she knew, had always loved the Stanhope place here on Grand Isle, and now she could easily see why. The house perched atop a bluff that dropped down to the lakeshore. It was painted a spruce green almost as dark as the firs beyond the clearing it centered and was two-storied, with a large circular turret at either end.

The road now merged into a driveway, which formed a crescent, and Karen followed it, parking at the end. Lilac bushes bloomed on either side of the front entrance, showers of purple and white blossoms suffusing the fresh, cool air with a wonderful scent. She took a deep breath, which made her somewhat heady, and all at once was glad that she had come here. Sorry that Maida was evidently in some sort of trouble, to be sure, yet glad that she had responded to her plea for help.

She pressed the doorbell, waited, then when no one responded after a time raised the rather ornate knocker—bronze, emblazoned with a family crest—and let it thud.

At this the door opened so suddenly that she nearly stumbled backward, glancing in apprehension at the man who stood before her. He was a total stranger to her, but this wasn't what bothered her. Rather it was the look in his eyes that frightened her. They were very light eyes, greenish, reminding her of a peridot she had once seen in a jeweler's window, devoid of any trace of yellow. She had wanted it because she had been born in August, and so it was her birthstone.

He was tall, she had to look up at him and she was slightly above average height. And it was with an effort that she wrested her gaze away from those disturbingly hostile eyes only to find herself concentrating on his equally disturbing, extremely male physique, this quite despite herself.

He was broad-shouldered, slim-waisted, and narrow-hipped, all of these physical attributes that tended to underline masculinity. But she was aware of much more than that. She sensed a restlessness, a tension, a leashed energy that was turbulent in its impact, making her think of a caged tiger on the verge of breaking his confines and springing loose.

It was such a dominant impression that Karen took a step backward without knowing she was doing so until she had done it. She imagined that she saw a faint hint of contempt brush a mouth that, she realized now, was very mobile. His mouth actually was far more expressive than the rest of his face. His face bothered her as much as anything about him—and everything about him seemed to be bothering her! She could not at the moment even have said with accuracy whether he was ugly or handsome. For there was a rigidity to his expression and a menace to his features that eclipsed everything else.

Thoroughly flustered, she tried to gather up the fabric of her composure, only to find her attention now riveted on his hair. Though he was young—certainly not more than thirty, she decided—his hair was so shot through with gray that the effect of it was like thick pewter contouring a head that was, without question, exceptionally well formed.

The gray hair, like everything else about this disturbing stranger, gave her an odd sense of shock. She swallowed hard, forcing herself to rally, and started to speak, intending to ask for Maida. But he was watching her so intently that she found herself fumbling for even the simplest of phrases, and before she could say anything at all he anticipated her.

"Whatever it is," he told her coldly, "we don't want it."

Before she could answer him he shut the heavy door firmly in her face.

She had taken the wrong fork in the road. Karen had no doubt at all about that. But a miscalculation on her part, something that could have happened to anyone unfamiliar with the network of country lanes around here, was certainly no excuse for such blatant rudeness.

She stared at the door, which seemed very large just now. A real barricade. She didn't know when she'd been so thoroughly angry! She actually reached up a clenched fist, intending to pound until the ill-mannered gray-haired stranger came to answer the summons, determined to be fully ready to tell him what she thought of him!

Her pulse was pounding, and her cheeks felt so hot she knew they must be flaming. She was shaking, literally shaking.

She assumed that he'd thought she was a saleswoman, but this did nothing to mitigate her feelings. She knew from her own experiences that having someone try to sell you something on a door-to-door basis could be exasperating, because sometimes such salespeople were very persistent and it was hard to make them take no for an answer. But she'd always recognized the fact that people had to make their living in a variety of ways, and so she had, at least, been polite about her refusals.

It occurred to her now that the gray-haired stranger probably didn't give a damn about the ways in which people made their living... or about much of anything at all!

Her fist about to strike the wood, Karen paused, and although her emotions were still at a fever pitch, logic came to insert a slender wedge of reason. She was in no shape at all right now to confront this man. She could imagine tumbling words out at him that would only create a verbal chaos. Certainly she needed to get considerably more control of herself than she had at the moment before she attempted to confront him—and even then it would be foolish. She couldn't imagine him laughing at her because she didn't think he had any laughter in him. But she flinched as she did imagine how searing his expression would become, and she had no desire to find out the real measure of his contempt.

Still standing in front of the door, she slowly began to pull herself together, although the encounter had left her ridiculously weak-kneed. Then, as her pure, primitive fury abated, she found herself wondering about him, wondering what possibly could have motivated him to behave as he had.

Why had he been so hostile? Maybe he'd been in the midst of something important to him and she had interrupted it; she could credit that. But even so, there had been no need for a display of such seemingly personal antagonism. Or, did he simply hate everybody?

She shook her head, unable to come to any satisfactory conclusions, and with one last look at the door, which now seemed like a fortress in itself, went back to her car.

As she turned the key in the ignition switch, she wondered if the bad-tempered stranger might be watching her from one of the windows facing this way, if only to make sure that she took her leave. But she doubted it. She doubted he'd bother.

Karen sighed, because the whole encounter was not only infuriating but oddly unsatisfactory as well. It left her with the sense of something unfulfilled...if only the chance to vent her opinion of him even though she was sure too that this was something else about which he couldn't care less!

She started up the road, driving slowly, and upon reaching the fork swung to the left. This time she came upon a house that very well could once have been a farmhouse. It was long and low with big chimneys and fields stretching beyond it where cattle must have grazed in earlier days.

And, this time, there was welcome. Maida came running out a side door and down a short flight of steps to clutch her and hug her as if she never wanted to let her go. Maida was almost crying in her excitement, and Karen found it hard to suppress her own tears, for she'd still not gotten back to her normal emotional level after this recent experience with the gray-haired stranger.

She followed Maida into a spacious pine-paneled living room furnished with maple and chintz-covered sofas and armchairs. The room overlooked the lake, and Karen took a long, appreciative look at the glorious view, then turned her attention to the fire blazing on the hearth. Although it was June the weather was still cool, but this was not the real reason why Karen went over to the fire and held out her hands, savoring its warmth. She was finding that she felt strangely chilled, in the wake of the anger that had, of necessity, remained unfocused.

Who *was* the pewter-haired man, in whose peridot-green eyes flaming hate and icy coldness seemed able to mix in disconcerting proportions?

Maida said, "Darling, this calls for a drink."

Karen raised her eyebrows. "It's not even four o'clock."

"But we're finally together again," Maida said. "It's been ages. Years. I was adding up. It really *has* been years. Before the—" She hesitated.

"Crash." Karen supplied the word for her. "Yes. Over a year before, wasn't it?"

"Yes. And then only for lunch, remember, when I went down to New York for a couple of days. Actually it's more like five years since we've been together for any length of time. In Florida when you and Keith had only been married a year or so and you were between concerts and we all got together for that week on Marathon Key. That was fun, wasn't it?"

Maida, Karen realized, was not merely talking, she was chattering. She looked at her cousin closely. She was still beautiful, with that copper hair and those incredible blue eyes, but tense. Very tense.

"Maida, why is Jerry in Boston, and why are you up here by yourself? And what is it that frightened you so badly you wanted me to rush up here?" she demanded.

Maida drew a long breath and smiled. "That's my Karen," she said. "Coming right to the point. The direct approach." Then her smile faded. "Jerry is in Boston and I'm up here because... we're going to get a divorce."

It was like a physical blow.

In Karen's opinion, Maida and Jerry had always been a perfect couple, unlikely though this might at first seem. Jerry, the Boston lawyer, was staid on the surface but wonderfully human underneath, and Maida, whom he had met while she was in a pre-Broadway tryout in Boston, was a talented actress, unpredictable, his complete antithesis. They had fallen totally in love, and it was a love, Karen had felt—especially as she saw her own marriage beginning to dissolve— that could be counted upon to last.

She sat down in a wide, floral-patterned armchair and said, "I think I'll take that drink."

"Vodka and tonic?"

"Anything."

"Be right back," Maida said. "The bar's in the kitchen."

Karen nodded and tried to shut out thought for the moment and to concentrate upon the view. It was really beautiful, with the aquamarine lake, the Adirondacks—some still snowcapped—in the distant background, and the spiky little islands offshore, fir covered, but evidently sheer stone to the water's edge. One of the islands looked quite close, though admittedly water distances were deceiving, and she thought it would be fun to explore it. She wondered if Maida had a boat, and if her arm would be strong enough for rowing, even so.

There was a long strip of dark-sanded beach directly below the windows, which had been cultivated as such, she suspected, for it soon became pebble-strewn in a path that stretched in both directions. The path, she knew, must go by the other house; the two places were probably not that far apart. The bends in the road had been deceptive.

There was a boat, down on the lakefront to the left. Did it belong to the other house or to Maida? she wondered, and almost at once got her answer. A man appeared quite suddenly, and she realized that there must be steps down the bluff that led from the other house to the lake and were hidden from her view by the trees.

Karen recognized him at once. He was wearing jeans and a green shirt, and there was a certain set to his broad shoulders and something indefinably tantalizing about the way he walked. He moved with an easy grace, yes. Somehow, she would have expected this. But it seemed to her that there was also an almost tangible defiance about his stance; surprisingly she got an impression of both hauteur and a kind of isolation, as if he were setting himself apart from the rest of the world.

Watching him, she smiled to herself. She was reading a great deal into very little and she wondered why she bothered. The hostile stranger surely had made his opinion of her more than abundantly clear. If she had any sense at all she would simply hope that while up here visiting Maida she didn't have another occasion to encounter him. That, certainly, would be for the best all the way around. Karen lifted her chin as if facing an invisible audience. There was one thing for certain. She wasn't about to put up with that kind of rudeness twice!

She tried to concentrate on something else, then felt her gaze pivoting back to him, and as she watched, he walked toward the boat. She saw him untie something, a rope she imagined, and then he started pushing the boat toward the water. The sun was starting its downward course. Though still high in the sky it was spilling bronze light over the lake and over the shorefront, and now it caught him within its aura so that momentarily it was as if he'd been highlighted. The light silvered his hair and etched his body with a golden outline, and watching, Karen caught her breath.

Someone else appeared on the scene. A boy. The sun finding an affinity in his yellow hair turned it to gold. He ran to the boat and helped the man push it into the water. Karen frowned. She imagined that the boy must be twelve or so. Ten, anyway. And the rude stranger, despite the gray hair, certainly didn't seem old enough to have a son that age. Perhaps the boy was a younger brother.

The boat was in the water now. They both climbed in, and the man picked up the oars, beginning to row with slow, even strokes. His course took him across the front of Maida's house, not all that far offshore.

As he passed directly in front of the living room windows, he looked up, and Karen instinctively shrank back. She could not see his expression clearly, not from this distance, but she wondered if he could see her at all here in the window. Did the sun possibly highlight her too? Or would she merely be a blur to him? Whichever, she had the sense that he was spying on her, and this made her uncomfortable.

But it was ridiculous to even imagine such a thing,

she told herself sharply, watching as he veered away from shore and started to row out toward the nearest island.

She heard the telephone ring, heard Maida's voice in answer, and then Maida came to the doorway and said, "For you, Karen."

For her? Who? she wondered, going out to the kitchen, then, when she lifted the receiver and heard Hugh MacKnight's voice, told herself that she might have known.

"I had to make sure you got there safely," Hugh said.

She laughed. "Well, I did."

"The driving went all right?"

"Fine."

He said triumphantly, "I told you it would." He had a right to be triumphant, she reminded herself. In a sense, the arm was as much his as it was hers.

"Don't overdo," he said, the doctor in him surfacing.

"I won't."

"You can't expect that arm to hold up if you put too much strain on it. Not yet. But in time..."

"Yes, Doctor," she teased.

Hugh chuckled. "It's second nature," he told her. Then, his voice lowered, "I miss you."

She skirted around this one and said lightly, "Want me to come back to work tomorrow?"

"Don't ask foolish questions," said Hugh, but she'd achieved her purpose. They finished the conversation on a pleasant yet relatively impersonal plane. Still, when she hung up, she turned to find Maida looking at her speculatively.

"The doctor you've been working for?" Maida asked.

"Yes," Karen nodded.

"Quite a conscientious employer, isn't he?"

Karen hesitated. "He's also a dear friend."

"More than that?"

"There can't be. He's married. And I don't feel that way about him."

A simple answer, but it gave the whole message.

They took their drinks, went back to the living room. Karen's eyes flew to the window. The boat had disappeared from sight. Had he put back in then, while she was talking on the phone? She surveyed the waterfront. No rowboat. Which must mean that he and the boy had gone around to the other side of the island.

Karen settled back into the same chintz-covered armchair and said to her cousin, "Now, tell me."

Maida, oddly hesitant, curled up in another armchair, also facing the window. "Funny, now that you're here, it isn't that easy. Nothing *dramatic* happened between Jerry and me."

Maida struggled for words and Karen, who had learned quite a bit about this sort of struggle in the past two years, let her seek to find them.

"Ever since Chad was killed..." Maida began, and Karen remembered. She had been on concert tour in San Francisco at the time when the word came. Keith had called her from New York to say that Maida had phoned that evening from Boston. And Maida had been terribly upset. Gerald Stanhope's younger brother, Chad, had been murdered.

Murdered.

"I was so shocked, Maida. It must have been a ghastly time for you."

"It was," said Maida, her lovely face unhappy as she, in her turn, remembered. "Chad was so young, only twenty-four, in med school and doing so well at it. He would have been a wonderful doctor. Jerry adored him. Jerry's five years older, but they'd always been inseparable. Jerry decided on law, then later Chad decided on medicine. Their father was so proud of both of them. Chad's death broke him—he was on the verge of remarrying, and the boys were pleased. He had been so alone since their mother's death. But the whole thing fell apart. He's still at our embassy in London, but I think after this tour of duty he'll retire. Then—I don't know. I have the feeling he'll just... crumble."

Maida spread her hands wide in a singularly graphic gesture. It was a way she'd always had, a method of expressing herself that had made people say, from the time she was a child, that she was a natural actress.

"Certainly Jerry isn't about to crumble," Karen said.

"In a way, he has," said Maida. "Not physically, of course. But I suppose you'd call it spiritually. First there was just a little crack between us and then it started to widen, and now it's a chasm. I've watched it grow, it was like standing and watching the earth opening up at your feet, the gap getting wider and wider. And there's nothing you can do; after a while you stop trying."

"Is there someone else?"

"For Jerry, or for me?" Maida smiled, a bitter little smile. "Not really," she said. "Though we've both tried. I knew that Jerry was seeing someone else, so I went out once or twice myself with a man I've known for years. But turnabout isn't always fair play, at least it isn't always satisfactory. It wasn't for me. So, instead, I'm going back to work."

"The theater?"

Maida nodded. "Yes, I've had offers. In the fall I plan to take one of them. But just now I needed to breathe," Maida said. "That's why I came up here a week ago; I've always loved it here."

"And?" Karen asked.

"And?"

"Well, something frightened you, you said that. That's why you wanted me to come up here so badly, remember?"

Maida's blue eyes clouded. "I'm not likely to forget," she said. "It's because of Michael. When I came up here, I didn't know that he'd be here."

"Who is Michael?"

"Michael Stanhope," said Maida. "Jerry's cousin." She gestured toward the window, toward the left, toward the direction of the other house. She said, "He's come back. They let him out." And, as Karen shook her head, not comprehending, she added, "It was Michael who killed Chad."

Chapter Three

Karen had noticed for months that in moments of stress, emotional as well as physical, it seemed as if an extra weakness crept over her arm, extending to her hand. Now she very nearly dropped the glass she had been holding, then quickly transferred it from her right to her left hand.

She stared at Maida, her thoughts whirling. "Is he tall?" she asked. "And...expressionless, I guess you'd say? And is his hair mostly gray?"

"Yes." Maida nodded, puzzled. "How did you know? You've never met him, have you?"

Karen smiled grimly. "Met him? No. And I don't think I ever want to, if I'm to judge from our first encounter. I took the wrong fork in the road on my way here and I—"

"Oh, God," Maida interrupted, "you must have wound up at the judge's house."

"The judge?"

"Jerry's uncle. What happened?"

"Michael Stanhope—it must have been he, wouldn't you say?—answered the door. Then he just stared at me as if I were the ultimate intruder for what seemed like forever but, I suppose, wasn't very long at all in actuality. And then, before I had the chance to ask if you were around, he—he slammed the door in my face." The memory still stung. "Maida, he seemed so angry! I've never encountered such intense dislike from anyone, much less a stranger."

Maida nodded. "Ever since Michael came back here he's been so hostile that I, for one, think he's positively demented, really psycho. For that matter, I didn't think that they should have considered him sane at the time it—it all happened." Maida faltered slightly on this. "But they did all sorts of testing and the psychiatrists said he was competent—I think that's what they called it—to stand trial."

"I don't like stirring up painful memories," Karen said slowly, "but it was a while after it happened before I came back to this country, a year or so later, then there was my own accident. I've never really known the whole story."

"Well," Maida said, "it was just after the Christmas holidays, three and a half years ago now. Chad was in medical school in Boston. Michael is Jerry's age, he must be thirty-two now, and at that time he was already a doctor, doing his surgical residency at a Boston hospital. Michael's father—Jerry's uncle—was a Superior Court judge in Massachusetts then. This pretty much wrecked the poor man, but I'll go into that later.

"Anyway, it was early January, and Rod Kensington, who is a cousin of both Michael's and Jerry's, was in Boston on a visit from Texas. On his last night Chad gave a farewell party for him. Rod's up here now incidentally, so you'll meet him. He's quite a charmer.

"His twin sister, June, was in Boston too. They both went to Chad's party, and there were quite a few others there, mostly friends of Chad's. I've been told it was late in the evening when Michael arrived. He had been on duty in the emergency room at the hospital.

"Rod and I were talking about this just a couple of days ago, as a matter of fact. Rod remembers that Michael seemed very tired when he got there, almost groggy. Evidently he had a couple of drinks in quick succession, and they really hit him. In fact Rod says that when he left with June, around midnight or so, Michael was asleep on a couch in the living room.

"It was about four o'clock in the morning when the police called Jerry. Since his father was in England, he was the first to be notified." Maida shuddered. "It was a nightmare," she said. "In fact, sometimes I find myself thinking that it really must have *been* a nightmare, but then I remember Chad is dead, and that's real enough."

"What happened?"

"Chad had a gun," Maida said tautly. "Ironically, it originally belonged to the judge—Uncle Doug, Chad and Jerry's uncle—but he gave it to Chad one summer when they were all up here because Chad liked to practice target shooting. Sometime after Rod and June left that night, Chad must have brought it out. We've never known why he did so. There was a girl named Susan Foster at the party who evidently had come with Michael, and later she testified in court. She said Michael simply took the gun, pointed it at Chad, and shot him."

Karen stared at her cousin in horror. "For no *reason*?"

"None that has been determined. Michael has insisted from the beginning that he had no memory of handling the gun at all, let alone firing it."

"Were there any other witnesses?"

"No. Just the Foster girl. She was a nurse at the hospital where Michael was doing his residency." Maida sighed. "The prosecution wanted to get an indictment on a first-degree murder charge," she said, "but the defense managed to have it changed to manslaughter. Michael was found guilty and sentenced to a state penitentiary for from five to ten years."

"But now he's free?"

"He's on parole. He was released last November."

The sun was lost to sight now, having disappeared behind the nearest island. In its gilded wake Karen could see a small boat round the distant rock-ledged corner.

Maida followed her gaze and said, "Yes, there he is. That's the Barnes boy with him. Ambrose. He's about the only person around here who associates with Michael, or perhaps I might better say with whom Michael will associate. I would think his parents would put a stop to it, though."

"What about the judge?" Karen asked "Do you think he knows his son is up here, living in his house?"

"He's living there himself," Maida answered. "He's been here on Grand Isle for nearly a year; he stayed right through the winter. He came here straight from the hospital, and Michael evidently joined him as soon as he was able to do so."

Maida sighed. "I haven't been over to see Uncle Doug since I arrived, and I really must go," she said, "but I'm wondering if I'll get any better reception from Michael than you did."

"You said the judge came here right from the hospital. Had he been ill?"

"He was in a terrible automobile accident not long after Aunt Eleanor died. The business with Michael, of course, took a dreadful toll too."

"Who was Aunt Eleanor?"

"His wife." The boat was coming closer now, they could see a figure rowing that even in this light seemed particularly rigid.

"Eleanor Stanhope was quite a person," Maida said softly. "After Michael was sent to prison, though, she just...collapsed. They said it was her heart, a condition she'd had for a long time, so maybe it was inevitable. Michael's trial and conviction certainly didn't help her, though."

"Was Michael her only child?"

"I suppose you'd say so," Maida conceded. "Actually, Eleanor and the judge never had any children of their own. That's what makes it especially ironic. They had chosen Michael. He was adopted."

A doorbell rang, and a man's voice called out, "Hey, am I interrupting something?"

"Rod," Maida said, and laughed and got to her feet.

The young man who came into the living room was not much taller than Maida, but his broad shoulders and tapered waist made him look like an athlete. He had a shock of blond hair, arresting gray eyes, and a quick smile.

Maida made introductions, and as Rod Kensington took Karen's hand he was openly appreciative. Karen found herself smiling back at him, but even while they exchanged pleasantries her mind was tallying up another message. This was the cousin from Texas who had been at Chad Stanhope's party the night he was shot.

"Will you be staying awhile?" he asked her now.

"Just till Maida gets acclimated," Karen told him.

Rod laughed. "Acclimated?" he asked. "If Maida isn't used to this place by now she never will be!"

"I don't know about that," Maida said quickly. "I'm a city girl. Night noises in the country frighten me."

"That makes two of us," Karen admitted.

"Well," Rod told them, "if the hoot owls and the crickets become alarming, just shout." He pointed to a clump of spruce trees past the clearing on the right. "You can't see it from here, but my cottage is just beyond those trees, Karen. I'm between you and my uncle, which makes me your nearest neighbor, I'm happy to say."

He sobered. "Maida, there isn't anything wrong, is there?"

"No, of course not," Maida said, almost too firmly.

He was looking at her thoughtfully. "Perhaps we should rig up some sort of alarm system."

"A long string, perhaps?" Maida suggested lightly. "You could tie it around your big toe when you go to bed at night, and if we get frightened, we can tug on it."

They laughed and let it go at that. Rod told them he had come over to say that he was going into Burlington in the morning to do some errands and would stop by before he left in case there was something they wanted. Meantime, he wondered if Maida could spare a couple of eggs.

She could, and as he followed her out to the kitchen Karen found herself turning toward the window again.

The boat had touched shore. Now the boy scrambled out of it, then the man followed, and they both tugged the boat to higher ground.

As she watched them Rod and Maida came back into the room, Rod holding an egg in each hand. He started to speak to her, then he too looked out toward the lakefront and his face darkened.

"Michael, damn him!" he said bitterly. "The only bad part of being up here is knowing that he's here too—though God knows he doesn't get in anyone's way if he can help it!"

"How is Uncle Doug?" Maida asked. "I tell myself each day that I must go over and see him, but I haven't been able to face it so far."

"I don't drop in on him too often myself, with Michael on the scene," Rod admitted. "I think the judge would be glad to see you, though, Maida." He turned to Karen. "My uncle," he said, "is a wonderful man who has had more than his share of tragedy."

Maida hesitated, then asked, "Can he walk at all?"

"No," Rod said tersely. "He's paralyzed from the waist down. He does remarkably well with his wheelchair, but it still hurts to see him like that."

"What does he do with himself?"

Rod shrugged. "I suppose you could say he creates

projects to fill in the hours. He's into geology at the moment, working over Aunt Eleanor's rock collection. Aunt Eleanor," he explained to Karen, "was quite a scientist."

Rod gestured toward the lakefront where Michael Stanhope and the boy with him were still lingering, skimming stones out across the water.

Rod said, "But for *him*, Aunt Eleanor would be alive today. Michael as much as killed her too."

After a while Rod took his eggs and left, and Maida offered Karen another drink.

Karen shook her head. "Not yet. I'd like to unpack first so the wrinkles will start shaking out."

The bedroom to which Maida showed her was on the left side of the house, facing the spruce trees that Rod Kensington had indicated, with a sliver view of the lake. It was papered in a pattern of violet nosegays, the purples and the blues repeated in the bedspread and the ruffled curtains at the window. Karen said, "It's charming. And that bed looks so comfortable! I think I could sleep for hours."

"I hope you'll be able to," Maida said abruptly.

Karen laughed. "I can't imagine any reason why not!" She turned quickly, surprised to find a strange expression on Maida's face. Fear? "Maida, what is it? You've never finished telling me what frightened you so badly that you called and literally begged me to come up here."

Maida shook her head, obviously reluctant. "Nothing, really."

"*Nothing?*"

"Loneliness, partly," Maida confessed.

"Loneliness isn't the same thing as fear."

"Well," Maida said, "I think it can breed fear.... All right, there *is* more to it than that. When I decided to come up here, I called Sam Landry. He's a jack-of-all-trades, he does painting, carpentry work, all sorts of things for Jerry, and usually he's kept his eye on the place when there's no one around.

"At that point I had to get away from Boston, from Jerry, from everything. At first I wasn't even going to tell Jerry where I was going. But in the end I left a note for him. However, I came without a key. That is, Jerry has one key to the house here and Sam has the other. So it was no particular problem; I simply stopped by at Sam's on my way—his place is down the highway a mile or so—and he offered to come on out here with me, but I told him there was no need. He gave me the key and that was that. He'd started the furnace for me, and his wife had seen to it that there was coffee and milk and some breakfast rolls on hand. I was exhausted. There were some cans of soup too. I heated one up and ate it and then I went to bed, even though it was early, and like you, I felt as if I could have slept forever."

"But something happened?"

"Yes," said Maida. "I woke up. I don't know what time it was. Late. There was someone in the room with me."

She shivered. "He had a flashlight and he was coming toward the bed. I just lay there with my eyes tightly closed. I could *feel* the light from the flash sweep over my face. Then it went away. Finally I dared to open my eyes again. There was just enough light so that I could see the figure of a man."

"What did he do?"

"Nothing," said Maida. "He went back out through the living room and I . . . well, I slipped out of bed and followed him. The phone's in the kitchen, as you know. We've never had an extension put in our room; we never wanted it. Now, though, I've gotten in touch with the phone company and they're going to put in another phone for me as soon as they can get to it. People don't rush things up here!"

"And the man," Karen persisted. "Do you know who he was?"

Maida nodded. "Michael Stanhope," she said. "He went out the kitchen door and headed around the front of the house, toward the steps that lead to the lakeshore. He had to switch on his flashlight to find the steps and it gave enough light so that I got a good look at his face."

"But what was he doing?"

Maida said bleakly, "I've no idea—and I'm not about to ask him! Needless to say I was praying every instant he was in the room, holding my breath. Just hoping that if I stayed still enough he'd believe I was asleep. He did, thank God. Otherwise—" Maida hesitated. Then she finished nervously, "There's no way of knowing what might have happened."

Karen felt a wave of shock wash over her. Maida was excitable, true, yet for all her surface frivolity she'd always had a good head on her shoulders and she'd never been one to scare easily.

"Maida, you don't seriously think that he came here with the intention of harming you, do you? And then for some reason changed his mind?"

"I don't think anything at all," Maida said firmly. "I just know that I realized I couldn't possibly stay here in the house by myself while Michael is next door, that's all."

"Perhaps you should...talk to him about this," Karen said slowly.

Maida stared at her as if she'd lost her mind. Then she said firmly, "No way! All I want is distance between us, and I think he'll keep his distance now that you're here. I don't think we'll find him doing any more prowling in this direction. There's safety in numbers, after all. At least that's what I'm counting on!"

Karen hung up the fleecy pink robe she had brought with her, having realized that early summer evenings were still apt to be chilly in northern Vermont. Then she said, "Maybe you should speak to Judge Stanhope about this."

Again Maida looked at her as if she'd lost her mind. Then she said flatly, "I wouldn't even consider doing such a thing. For one thing, the judge certainly has enough troubles of his own. Just having to put up with having Michael around must be a major one. And if I were to speak to the judge and Michael were to find out...well, there's no saying what something like that might trigger."

Karen was quiet for a moment, unpacking slowly in an effort to stall, while she thought about all of this. She could understand Maida's fear of Michael Stanhope; she remembered only too well the searing green gaze, the defiant hostility. That was the word. She lingered on it. Michael had been defiant as well as angry, he had acted like a person trying to protect himself from....

From what? she wondered. The world? Very possibly so. If he had been suffering from some sort of mental blackout at the time of Chad's murder and yet had been convicted for it and served time in prison as a result, his bitterness would be something easy enough to understand. And his hostility.

Strange, but now that she thought about it, it seemed to her that there also had been a certain vulnerability in back of his attitude. Although his actions remained unforgivable, this did put things in a slightly different context.

Still being careful with her word choice, she said, "Maida, I can see that he frightens you—"

"Yes," Maida interrupted. "As a matter of fact he terrifies me!"

"Do you think the judge would really have him living here if he were... a dangerous person? I should think that he, of all people, wouldn't want another tragedy to occur. I admit it seems very strange, Michael Stanhope coming in here in the night like that. But don't you think there's a chance that there might be some logical explanation?"

Maida stared at her, and then she said, "I don't believe you, Karen. You've told me how he greeted you when you went to his house by mistake!"

"True. But even so... what I'm trying to say is that it seemed to me you may be... overreacting just a bit, darling. From what you've said, Michael Stanhope isn't a criminal. Not in the true sense of the word. True, from what you've said he did commit a terrible crime, but evidently he wasn't in possession of his faculties at the time and—"

"He was found competent to stand trial," Maida put in.

"Even so...."

"I know. All right, it *does* seem as if he was either drunk or stoned or both at the time. Even so, he was convicted and sent to prison. And I think if the judge hadn't been in that accident Michael would still be there. The judge has a lot of connections, a lot of friends. I think they went to bat for him in regard to getting Michael paroled because they felt the judge needed him. As for Michael himself... I don't know. Maybe he isn't actually *dangerous*. Maybe I'm blaming him for at least part of what's happened to Jerry and me. But you've got to admit that he's strange at the least. You had a brief taste of what he's like this afternoon."

She shrugged. "Enough of that," she said. "It's time for another drink, and then some supper. I bought one of Mrs. Barnes's chicken pies—wait till you taste it."

"Ambrose's mother?" Karen asked.

"You catch on fast." Maida smiled. "That's right. The Barneses run the general store down on Route Two, and she bakes to order on the side. People have to put their hand to a lot of things in places like this in order to make a living."

Karen closed her suitcase, stashed it in a corner. She followed her cousin out to the kitchen. Going through the living room, she glanced almost cautiously toward the lakeshore. It flamed now with the golden magnificence of the setting sun, but there was no one there. No man, no boy. Only the boat.

Chapter Four

When Rod Kensington stopped by the next morning he invited Karen to drive into Burlington with him. She was hesitant, but Maida urged her to do so. "Go ahead, it's a gorgeous day," she insisted, "and I have several letters to write."

It was cool, so she borrowed a coat from Maida and took her place in the front seat of Rod's yellow sports car. Last night she had dreamed again, the old familiar nightmare but with an added note. At the last moment it had been Michael Stanhope, rather than Keith, smiling that odd smile that continued to haunt her. As it usually did, the nightmare left her feeling tired, and so she was not as responsive to Rod as she might have been, for he was, admittedly, a very engaging young man.

They shopped, then on the return trip Rod insisted upon taking her to lunch at a pleasant colonial-style restaurant.

As they studied the menu he said accusingly, "I've the feeling you haven't really been with me this morning."

"I'm sorry," she said wryly, then admitted, "I didn't sleep well."

"Does being in a strange place keep you awake?"

"No, not necessarily."

"Nothing disturbed you, did it?"

"What do you mean?" she hedged.

"Maida told me about Michael prowling around her first night on Grand Isle. I don't *think* it's anything to be worried about, but there's no saying what the better part of three years in prison did to him, Karen."

Karen hesitated only briefly, then plunged. "You were at Chad's party, weren't you?"

"Yes," Rod said soberly. "I was. My sister and I left before it happened, though, and ever since, I've wondered if I could have gotten hold of the gun myself, if I'd stayed."

The waitress came to take their orders, and when she had left, Karen, seeing the somber note in Rod's gray eyes, said, "I'm sorry. I shouldn't have asked you about it."

"It happened," Rod said tersely. "Unfortunately, it's a memory that can't be erased."

"And... there's no doubt about Michael's guilt?"

"I don't see how there can be. Despite Michael's insistence that he never touched the gun, there doesn't seem to be any doubt about it. There *was* a witness."

"Have you ever spoken to Michael about it?"

Rod's glance was horrified. "My God, no! In fact Michael and I haven't spoken much about anything since I came up here a week ago, and that's the first time I'd seen him since the trial. As June and I were both at the party, we had to testify."

He hesitated, then evidently decided to confide in her. "I'm only up here because of my mother," he said. "The cottage belongs to her—she's the judge's sister, as you may already know—but she's lived in San Antonio for a number of years now and she has no desire to come to Grand Isle anymore. She is interested in selling the place, and since I had to be in New York on business late last month she asked if I'd come on up and look into the situation for her. I had no idea Michael was out of prison, nor, especially, that he was on Grand Isle."

"When did you find out?" Karen asked him.

"The day after I arrived, when I went over to see my uncle. It was enough of a shock to have a bodyguard, who looks like a thug, open the door. Then I discovered Michael was there as well."

"The judge has a bodyguard?"

"Probably he's some sort of male nurse," Rod admitted. "Uncle Doug is quite helpless, he does need care, but I would think the reason Michael is there at all might be to look after him. On the other hand, Uncle Doug may have had his own ideas about that."

The waitress brought them the delicious broiled lake fish they had ordered, and as they ate, Rod made an obviously deliberate effort to change the subject. Karen went along with it, asking him questions about Texas and his life there. He was, she learned, with an oil company.

"Not all desk work, either," he told her. "I have my chance to get out into the field at times, to be where the action is."

They were both rather silent on the drive back to Grand Isle, and when they came to the fork in the road Karen instinctively flinched as she remembered yesterday and her encounter with Michael Stanhope.

Maida had indeed been spending her time writing

letters, and shortly after Rod went back to his cottage she decided to take them up to the post office and mail them. Left alone, Karen hesitantly approached the steps that led down to the lakefront. She wanted to walk along the shore and to lose herself in the beauty of her surroundings, yet she had no desire at all to trespass upon the property next door. Still, there was a path along the lakefront in both directions, so she struck out to the left, glad that she had thought to put on sneakers before starting on this safari. The path was a rough one, for the lakeshore, as she had noted from the window, was strewn with stones that ranged from pebbles to good-size rocks, except for the beach area directly in front of the house.

The pine-scented air was marvelously bracing, and she drew in great, stimulating drafts of it. After a time she paused to sit down on a large flat boulder and discovered that she finally was beginning to unwind. Natural beauty was a tonic, there was no doubt about it. The serenity of the distant snowcapped Adirondacks gave her a sense of endurance, of stability. There was a permanency to mountains. She didn't wonder at Maida coming up here to sort out her problems, for this was a place in which one really *could* get away from it all—or could one? Even as she thought this Karen heard twigs snap behind her and a pebble rolled across the ground, coming to rest at her feet.

She sprang up, startled, and turned to face the intruder, recognizing him at once. Ambrose.

He was a sturdy youngster, with a shock of yellow hair, bright blue eyes, and a tilted nose enchantingly sprinkled with freckles. For an instant he looked as startled as she did, then he grinned.

"You're the lady next door," he said.

"No," she said, "that's my cousin."

Ambrose shook his head. "I don't mean her," he said. "You're the *new* lady next door. Since yesterday. Your cousin told my mom about you when she bought the chicken pie."

"Well," said Karen, laughing.

"You going or coming?"

"I'm about to start back."

"Then I'm heading your way," Ambrose told her. He must, she thought, be twelve or so; he was taller than he had seemed from the window. He said, "You staying long?"

"Just a few days."

"Too bad," said Ambrose. "The fishing's getting good, and school'll be out pretty soon. Then I could take you—mornings, that is. If you like fishing."

She remembered going fishing years ago, with her father. She said softly, "It's been a long time."

"Well," said Ambrose practically, "it's not something you forget."

"I suppose not."

He stopped, picked up a stone, skimmed it out over the water.

"How do you do that?" Karen said. "There must be a trick to it."

"Kind of," he conceded. He searched for the right size, the right shape, among the rubble of pebbles at his feet. He held it out to her, showing her how to hold it just so, with her thumb crooked, how to swing at just the proper angle. She followed instructions, but the stone plopped dismally, without skipping, without widening circles, as she said "Ouch."

There was genuine concern in the bright blue eyes. "What's the matter?" Ambrose asked.

"My arm," she said. "I hurt it quite badly a while back. It still isn't very strong."

"Then," Ambrose said, in an almost fatherly tone, "you'd best not try that again until it's better. Doesn't do to push things."

"No," she agreed, repressing a smile. "Sometimes it doesn't."

They walked along companionably, Ambrose telling her the names of some of the little islands offshore, pointing out the peaks of the distant Adirondacks, saying "That's Marcy," and "That's Whiteface." It seemed to her that it took only half the time to reach the beachfront by Maida's house than it had taken her to go alone in the other direction. Then her heart sank, for Ambrose suddenly called out, "There he is," and cupping his hands over his mouth to improvise a megaphone, he shouted, "Hey, Mike!"

Michael Stanhope was walking with his back to them, he must just have come down from his own house. Now he swung around, and as Ambrose tugged at her hand she felt herself captured, being drawn into the very situation she had hoped to avoid.

She said, "Ambrose, look, I'm right here at my cousin's, and I should go on up."

But he said, with a young boy's persistence, "No. You got to meet Mike. Maybe he'll let you go fishing with us. We're going to pack a picnic and go Saturday, if the weather's good."

She shrank back, but there was no avoiding a confrontation without making an issue of it. Michael Stanhope stood where he was, letting them come to him. *He doesn't want this meeting any more than I do,* she thought. *Perhaps even less!*

"Mike, this is the new lady," Ambrose said excitedly. "I found her up there a way, sitting on a rock."

Karen thought she saw amusement touch Michael Stanhope's face briefly, but it was such a fleeting thing that she wasn't sure. She felt herself drawn to his eyes once again, but today when she met them she saw no anger there. They were curiously expressionless; in fact, she felt as if she were looking through a window into an empty room.

Ambrose, glancing from one to the other of them, said to her, "Hey, I don't even know your name! But this is Mike Stanhope."

"I'm Karen Morse," she said reluctantly, and to her surprise Michael Stanhope nodded, very slightly.

"How do you do, Mrs. Morse," he said smoothly, with a politeness that was suspicious under the circumstances.

Mrs. Morse. It was the correct form of address, of course, but it made her wary at the moment. It meant that he knew who she was. Had he known this when he had shut his front door in her face? He also knew that she was married, or had been married, and he must also know that she was Maida's cousin. The thought of his knowing this much about her was disquieting.

She didn't want to hurt Ambrose's feelings, but the need to make matters clear eclipsed even that. She said, "Mr. Stanhope, Ambrose was rather insistent that I come along and meet you."

"Yes, I can imagine," he said, still with that grave politeness that had the effect of putting her on guard.

But then, to her surprise, he added tonelessly, "You needn't worry, Mrs. Morse. I didn't think it was your idea."

She could find no instant reply to this, and Ambrose promptly filled the conversational gap. "Mike," he said, "she hasn't fished for a long time but she says she likes it. I think she'd do all right if we helped her out. Could she come along with us Saturday?"

Michael Stanhope's lips twisted wryly. Then he said, "I doubt Mrs. Morse would enjoy our kind of fishing trip, Ambrose."

"But she would," Ambrose insisted. He turned to her, his freckled face appealing. "You would, wouldn't you?" he asked her.

Something perverse arose in Karen, an instinct she hadn't even known she possessed. To her own horror she found herself saying, "Yes, I would as a matter of fact. I'd like to come with you if you have room for me...and don't feel I'd be a nuisance."

"Gee," said Ambrose, "there's plenty of room, isn't there, Mike?"

Michael Stanhope's expression remained unchanged. "I don't know," he said. "In any event, we'll be leaving early. Probably too early for you, Mrs. Morse."

"I can set my alarm," she said sweetly and thought, *Why am I doing this? He could hardly make it plainer. He doesn't want me, I'd be a total intruder. And Ambrose—well, Ambrose may want me because, in a way, I'm a novelty to him. But he'd be just as happy alone with Michael.*

Looking down at Ambrose, she wondered if his

parents knew that Michael Stanhope was not long out of prison; they must, she supposed, yet they did not seem to hesitate to let their son spend a good deal of his spare time in Michael's company.

Feeling that she had taken entirely the wrong step, she said, "Ambrose, Mr. Stanhope is right. I know you'll both want to get a good start on the day, and it probably would be early for me. Maybe some other time."

"But you said you're not staying long," Ambrose protested, and now she *did* catch an expression on Michael Stanhope's face, but she could not quite read it. Relief, perhaps?

"I'll be back," she fibbed. "Maybe later in the summer, if my cousin stays up here."

Involuntarily she met Michael's eyes, and she flinched, despite herself. There was an expression of pure pain in them. But his tone was indifferent. "Is Jerry up here with Maida?" he asked.

"No," she said. "He stayed in Boston."

"I wondered..." he began, and then let the words trail into nothing.

He shrugged, ever so slightly, and said to Ambrose, "Look, you wanted to walk down to the Point to see if we could find Indian arrowheads. There won't be enough light left to look for them if we don't get going."

"Okay," Ambrose said and turned back to Karen. "Mrs. Morse, would you maybe like to—"

She interrupted swiftly. "Another time, Ambrose. Right now my cousin's expecting me."

She waved, a brief little wave that included both of them, and started up the steps, feeling that Michael

Stanhope's eyes were on her back, that they were boring into her.

For just a moment there had been something about him that reached out to her. A brief glimpse of anguish, yes, but something more as well. She wondered if he might have said anything else about Jerry if Ambrose had not been present.

Chapter Five

Maida awakened Friday morning with a miserable cold. It was an overcast day, the lake gunmetal, the clouds sullen. By noon it was raining, a heavy, pelting, early summer rain.

"It's good for the crops, I suppose," sniffed Maida, who had no interest whatsoever in crops. "Miserable for you, though, to be cooped up here with me. I hope you don't come down with this too! It feels like incipient pneumonia."

Karen could not suppress a smile. Maida was inherently dramatic.

After lunch Maida decided, after some prompting, to take a nap, and Karen settled down in an armchair with a mystery novel she'd found in a corner bookcase.

It was a clever story, yet she could not lose herself in it. She kept looking out the window, half expecting to see either Ambrose or Michael Stanhope or both of them stalking along, wearing heavy yellow slickers, having refused to let the weather daunt them in their daily walk. But she could have been alone in the world, for all the glimpses of other humanity the lakefront offered.

About four o'clock she brewed herself a cup of tea, and wished that there were cookies to go with it. Maida had an actress's conscience when it came to her figure, and kept a spartan cupboard except for occasional indulgences such as the chicken pie the other night. She opened the refrigerator. Maida should be drinking fruit juice and the supply was almost exhausted. And the aspirin bottle, standing on the drainboard, was empty.

Karen made an instant resolution and put it into action. She penned a quick note, "Gone for a few supplies," in case Maida should awaken before she returned, borrowed Maida's tangerine-colored raincoat and matching hat, and set forth. Just this morning Maida had said that they should go over to Burlington and turn the rental car in; no need for both of them to have cars here. She should have thought that out, she had said, and met Karen at the airport in Burlington in the first place. But Maida had a foreign car with a different sort of drive—strange enough, at least, so that Karen, still hesitant about her arm when it came to driving, didn't want to pioneer it. The rental car was fine, just a nice little American compact that was easy to handle, and she was glad now, that she'd kept it.

At the intersection of Route Two she turned toward South Hero and, within a mile, saw the general store at the side of the road, gas pumps out in front.

The man at the counter inside reminded her so much of Ambrose that she knew this must be his father. And despite the fact that he appeared very much the conventional taciturn Yankee, Mr. Barnes swiftly managed to elicit the fact that she was Karen Morse, Maida Stanhope's cousin, here to visit.

"Matter of fact," said Mr. Barnes, "my son Ambrose said he ran into you yesterday, down by the lake."

"Yes, he did," Karen admitted.

Mr. Barnes left his place behind the counter, coming with her to go over the available fruit juices with a view toward making a selection that would be "tasty" for Maida and at the same time do its part toward helping her cold. He said, opting first for a blend of grapefruit and pineapple juice, "Ambrose and Mike Stanhope are thick as thieves," and when she inadvertently looked her surprise, he added solemnly, "Don't pay too much heed to what you hear, Mrs. Morse. Mike Stanhope saved Ambrose's life this past winter, at the risk of his own. Ambrose had gone out on the lake to try his hand at ice fishing— his Mom and I had no idea what he was up to. Ice cracked, and he went through. Mike had just come back from getting some provisions here, heard someone yelling, and went right out after him. Wasn't no easy matter—ice would have carried him under too, then they'd both have been for it. But he used his head—lucky he's got a good one on his shoulders or we wouldn't have our son today. Guess you can understand there's not thanks enough we can ever give him. And our kid worships the ground he walks on. So does my wife." Mr. Barnes's eyes actually twinkled. "If I was a jealous man, now—"

The little bell over the door tinkled; another customer. Karen took her fruit juice, aspirin, and the box of chocolate-covered graham crackers she had added for her own selfish purposes and departed.

The rain was really slashing down now. The windshield wiper worked overtime, and still she could hardly see. She nearly passed the turnoff road, started down it, swearing at the potholes made worse than ever by this torrent, and was nearly to the fork when she saw a blur of orange through the windshield, that seemed to get larger and larger, coming ever closer. She veered crazily, trying to escape. She heard, rather than felt, the crash. And then there was nothing. . . .

Someone was saying, "Oh, my God! I was braking, I was just about *stopped* but I guess the rain distorted things so she thought I was coming right at her. She just swung to one side, she *threw* the car down into the gully. . . ."

Someone else said, "She'll be all right. Horace, get some brandy."

There was authority in the second voice and now there was authority in the first voice too, as the speaker said, "Not *yet,* Dad. Not till she's fully conscious." She could feel strong hands going over her body, probing tentatively, lifting. "Nothing broken, I'm pretty sure of that. Even so, there should be X rays. I think I'll take her into Burlington. . . ."

She opened her eyes and found herself staring directly into Michael Stanhope's face. But this was quite a different Michael Stanhope. Even though her head throbbed, even though she was more than a little dazed, she realized that.

Concern—if she'd had to find a single word to describe his expression, that would have been it. Concern or . . . tenderness? And there was something else in those arresting, light green eyes. A certain professionalism. But then, she remembered, he was, after all, a doctor.

Now he smiled very faintly, a crooked little smile that did strange things to Karen and she swallowed hard in an effort to keep the tears back. It was a futile effort, though, because suddenly tears filled her eyes anyway, and she found herself powerless to prevent them.

He said, "You're back with us." Then, seeing the tears, he added gently, "Hey, there's no need for that!" He produced a handkerchief and she took it out of his hands. In a most unglamorous manner, she blew her nose and then tried to sit up. But a firm hand restrained her.

"Not yet," he said. "Got that brandy, Horace?"

"Yes," someone said gruffly, and Karen looked up into the face of one of the ugliest men she had ever seen. He *did* look like a thug, or a gorilla, or a combination of the two.

Michael held the brandy, letting her sip only a little at a time. She nearly choked on the first sip and he cautioned, "Take it easy." And then, finally, he said, "Okay, you can try to sit up. But let me help you."

He put his arms around her and she clung to him as he eased her up gently until she was sitting in the corner of the couch with pillows propped at her back.

It was only then that she saw the third person. Although he was in a wheelchair, there was nothing of the invalid in his appearance. He was a fine-looking man with thick white hair, intensely blue eyes, and a vitality that seemed to negate his obvious helplessness.

He smiled at her reassuringly. "Hello, my dear, I'm

Judge Stanhope. This is Horace, my assistant. And I think you've already met my son, Michael."

"Yes," she said. "Yes, I have." Michael had stood back, but he was still looking down at her, and she asked, "Was it your car?"

She meant it as a question only, certainly not as an accusation, but she saw him tense, and she cried out quickly, "Look, I know it was my own stupid fault!"

He shook his head. "No. The road is unfamiliar to you and the rain was coming down in torrents. You'd put your headlights on, which was a good thing—they didn't help your visibility much, I'm sure, but I could see a reflection of your lights so I knew there was a car ahead and I braked." He drew a long breath. He said, "Let's just be thankful it wasn't any worse. I—I could have killed you."

The words seemed to echo in the sudden, intense silence that filled the room. In its wake the judge cleared his throat and said, "Michael, you spoke about taking Mrs. Morse into Burlington."

"Yes," Michael said. "I'd like to have someone else go over her. And there should be some X rays taken."

"I don't think it's necessary," Karen said quickly. "I may have a few bruises in the morning, but I honestly don't think I'll be that much the worse for wear. The car, though—what's happened to it?"

"A smashed front end," said Michael. "I think it will have to be towed. But that doesn't matter particularly. You do." He hesitated, then said, "If you don't want to go into Burlington with me, maybe Horace could take you. I'll phone ahead to the hospital."

"But why wouldn't I want to go with you?" she

asked, and stopped short when she saw the skeptical expression on his face. Hastily she said, "I just don't want to be such a—such a nuisance."

"Nor are you," the judge assured her smoothly. "Horace, help Michael get Mrs. Morse into the car, will you. Then go across and tell Mrs. Stanhope that her cousin has met with a slight accident but she's all right and will be home as soon as possible. No, on the other hand, I'll call Maida and tell her myself."

"I'll bring the car up to the door, Horace," Michael said.

Horace nodded. "I can carry you, miss, if you've no objection," he said. Then, before Karen could speak, he had reached down and gathered her up in strong, sinewy arms, holding her as if she were a feather.

The judge laughed at her expression. "Horace was a wrestler at one point in his career," he told her. "He handles me much the same way, my dear—and I weigh quite a few pounds more than you do!"

Horace tucked Karen into the front seat of the car with a gentleness that was completely at variance with his appearance, then wrapped a blanket around her legs and placed a pillow at her back.

Michael slanted an appraising green glance in her direction before he started the car up again, and she found herself shivering. This had nothing to do with being cold, certainly nothing to do with fear. Rather, she was so thoroughly conscious of the man sitting next to her that the effect was shattering. And she was remembering that singularly appealing, slightly crooked smile that had caused such a profound reaction, stirring her in a way that was unfamiliar and very, very emotional.

He said quickly, "You're not warm enough? I can switch on the heater."

"No," she said, her voice sounding surprisingly shaky. "I'm all right. Really."

He nodded and started up the driveway, handling the car with an easy competence. She found herself relaxing, momentarily at least. In some ways, she knew, it would be difficult to ever remain relaxed around Michael Stanhope. He had much too profound an effect on her. But, just now, she felt herself encased in the protective cocoon of his care, and it was a surprisingly reassuring feeling. He would take care of her, she knew he'd take care of her. She had absolute confidence in him.

This was instinctive. Intuition? She supposed you could call it that, but she wasn't a great believer in so-called feminine intuition. No, it was more than that. It was a very deep inner feeling.

This made it all the more disconcerting when, as they were going along the main road, he suddenly laughed, a mocking laugh, and said, "You look like a frightened mouse!"

Karen glanced at him quickly. The dashboard light etched his profile with cameo clarity, and she felt a catch in her throat. What a handsome man he was! Tragedy had left a certain mark on him, but even so....

He said abruptly, "I suppose you think I keep a gun in the glove compartment."

She gasped. It was as if he'd taken a glass of ice water and dashed it in her face. It wasn't even so much what he'd said—shocking though that was in itself when one knew his background—but the tone of his voice, for there was something deadly in it. Hatred?

She remembered again his hostility at their first encounter. She'd thought since that moment when she'd come back to consciousness in the judge's house that those first negative feelings were part of the past. But now she saw that she could not have been more wrong.

Overriding everything else, though, she sensed an underlying weariness in his voice, a hopelessness. And at the same time she realized that he was testing her in effect by making such a sudden, explosive statement, testing her in a way that most people would call sadistic. Karen didn't understand his reason for that, either. But then how could she expect to? It didn't take much insight to appreciate the fact that she could not really imagine how she, how anyone, must seem to Michael Stanhope. Three years in prison. That in itself was enough to take an incredible toll on a man.

She saw his hands clench the steering wheel, waiting for her answer. Baiting her—yes, he was baiting her, casting out to see what he might get back.

Karen said slowly, "If you keep a gun in your glove compartment, then you must have a valid reason."

He didn't answer but she felt as if a current had begun to flow between them, she could feel herself being caught up in it.

She leaned her head back against the pillow and closed her eyes. After a moment she heard him ask anxiously, "Are you all right?"

"Yes."

"Look, that was a stupid remark on my part." It

was as if the words were being wrung out of him.
"I'm sorry."

"It's all right," she said. And somehow it was.

In the dim light his profile was inscrutable. The
windshield wiper moved back and forth across the
glass in an hypnotic rhythm. It reminded her of her
metronome when, as a child, she had started to study
piano. *Tick-tock, tick-tock,* swing to this side, then that
side, to this side, then that side.

They passed through Winooski, crossed the bridge
into Burlington. Michael drove through the unfamiliar night to a building that she knew must be the hospital, the neon-lighted word "Emergency" leaping
out at her.

He told her to wait, and she watched him dash
through the rain, turning up the collar of his raincoat.
And again she closed her eyes, feeling terribly weary.

He came back and without a word started the car
and drove directly up to the emergency entrance
where a man in a white coat was waiting with a wheelchair. Karen wanted to protest, to tell them that she
wasn't a helpless infant but could perfectly well navi-
gate on her own. But Michael left her and she heard
him say something about parking.

She was wheeled down a long corridor, X-rayed,
taken into an examining room. A nurse took her
blood pressure, then there was a young doctor smiling
down at her.

"I'm Brad Simmons," he told her. And he added,
"I was in med school with Michael."

In med school with Michael. All at once the enormity
of everything that had happened to Michael Stanhope
swept over her; not merely the prison term, but the

end of his chosen career, loneliness, bitterness. No
wonder he seemed hostile, haunted.

Dr. Simmons moved her arm, and involuntarily
she flinched. He said, "The scars. What happened?"

She told him briefly: the accident, the subsequent
surgery. It wasn't until she had finished that she realized someone else had come into the room. Michael.

Brad Simmons looked across at him. He said, "I
think she'll do, Mike. We'll check the X rays, of
course, before we let her go. Tomorrow morning
you're going to feel as if you're made of aches and
pains, Mrs. Morse. I'll give you something. But in just
a couple of days—"

"Thank you," she said and started to sit up.

"Don't rush it," Dr. Simmons admonished her.
"Stay here with her, will you, Mike, while I check the
films?"

Michael crossed the room and stood beside the examining table. Then he said slowly, "I didn't know
about your arm."

She forced a smile. "There's no particular reason
why you should have."

"I wondered why you had stopped playing," he
told her, and when she looked surprised, he added, "I
went to a concert of yours once, in Boston. You played
Chopin for an encore. The critics inferred that it took
quite a bit of guts, since it was fashionable to look
down one's nose at the romantic school. But you'd
already proved that you could cope with Mozart—or
with Bartók or anyone else for that matter, of any
school, any era. I know relatively little about music,
but I liked that."

She was shaken by this statement, more shaken

than she wanted him to realize. Tentatively she slid her legs down to the floor and stood up. She wobbled, and Michael reached out an arm to steady her. She found herself leaning against his shoulder and the wish that they could prolong this moment and that she could stay in the shelter of his arm for a long long time swept over her. It seemed so natural to have him hold her like this. Years seemed to have passed since the first moment she'd seen him. But, thinking of the first moment, memory forced her to ask, "Why did you shut the door in my face the other afternoon?"

He hesitated and she was afraid he was suddenly going to shut himself off from her again. But then he said, "I honestly thought you were another female journalist, tracking down a story. I've been grist for their mills. It was bad enough in the beginning," he added bitterly, "but it got worse. After my mother died, after my father was in the accident, they even tried to get at me in prison. Then last fall, when I came back to Grand Isle to be with Dad, it was like having a bunch of vultures descend. They still show up every now and then."

"I see."

"It was an understandable mistake on my part," he told her. "Some of them are very attractive young ladies. Usually I don't answer the door. I leave that to Horace. But the other afternoon he was out with my father."

Dr. Simmons appeared so quietly that he was in the room before they were aware of him. "Nothing broken," he assured Karen. "Not even chipped, not even bent. Though that arm of yours presents an interesting picture."

"I can imagine it does," she said wryly.

"You must have had an excellent surgeon."

"I did," she told him. "Hugh MacKnight."

"Tops in the orthopedic field," Dr. Simmons conceded.

He walked with them to the emergency entrance and waited with Karen while Michael dashed through the rain to bring the car around. He said, watching Michael's retreating figure, "Do you know him well?"

"No." She laughed. "Intricate relationship—my first cousin married his first cousin."

Dr. Simmons was momentarily startled. "Chad?" he asked. "But Chad wasn't—"

"No," she said quickly. "Gerald. Chad's older brother."

He nodded soberly. "It was—it *is*—a terrible thing. Worse for Michael than anyone else—except Chad, of course, who should be alive and interning some place by now. And Michael should be well into his residency. Surgeons have a long one." He looked across at her. "Michael paid the price," he said. "The price demanded by law, that is. But the account sheet will never balance for him, will it? And that's not right, either."

His words trailed off as Michael drove up, and he helped her into the car. She said, "Thank you, very much."

"Would that all my cases were like you!" Dr. Simmons said.

Unexpectedly Michael smiled, and she caught her breath. The smile transformed him, revealing the potential of a personality she was only beginning to appreciate. Briefly, despite the gray hair, he looked younger than she would have believed possible. Then he laughed and said, "You haven't changed, Brad."

"No answer to that." Brad Simmons grinned and waved good-bye.

As they drove out of the parking lot, Karen said, "He was very nice."

"Brad?" Michael asked absently. "Yes, he is. He's also developed into a good physician."

There was a stop sign at the next corner. Michael braked the car, and the light from a corner streetlamp shone full upon him so that she could see his face clearly. His expression was unreadable, but it seemed to her that he could not fail to be thinking of himself and his own shattered career.

Because it seemed so vital to her she said, "You *are* going to go back into medicine yourself, aren't you?"

He gave her a look of pure scorn. "No," he said bluntly. "When something ends, there *is* no returning. It's like your plane crash, in its way. You can't bring your husband back, can you?"

It was said callously, the brutality was deliberate, and she shrank away from him. Then, after a moment, he said with cool indifference, "Now, I suppose I've made you cry again!"

Anger stabbed her. She said coldly, "No, you haven't. Is that what you wanted?"

They were passing a drive-in restaurant, and he swung abruptly into the parking lot. He stared down at her, and she realized that the indifference had been purely feigned; she suspected that there was much that was feigned in the harsh, sometimes brutal, front Michael Stanhope was apt to assume as a kind of armor.

Just now his face looked haggard and his eyes were fathomless. And the realization came to her that her accident must have been a particularly dreadful kind of ordeal for him. She recalled his words, spoken in his father's living room, "I could have killed you."

It was he who had found her unconscious, and how ghastly, how much more than ghastly, it must have been for him in that initial second when he may well have wondered if she were dead, this reviving memories too terrible for her even to begin to comprehend.

She remembered his concern as he had bent over her there in his father's house, and the gentle, expert probing of his fingers. Now the thought of his touch brought quite a different kind of sensation, and as she looked across at him she was totally conscious of the tremendous masculine appeal of this complex man, his hair turned gray long before its time.

He said, "I thought we both could use some coffee." Then, before she could speak, he was out of the car, and she watched his tall figure striding through the rain, entering the drive-in only to reappear, moments later, with cups of coffee for both of them.

They sat with the rain streaming down the windshield, shimmering with ever-changing patterns of green, blue, and red borrowed from the colored bulbs strung around the drive-in's roof. The coffee was bracing, but as she sipped it Karen was aware that she was, indeed, beginning to ache all over, just as Brad Simmons had predicted she would, and this was an indication that the protective cloak of shock following the mishap was wearing off.

She flinched as she moved her leg slightly, and Michael asked at once, "What is it?"

"Just a few assorted aches and pains," she said, deliberately making light of it, but nevertheless she saw a spasm of something close to pain cross his face.

"Dammit!" he said, so quietly she almost didn't hear him.

"Look," Karen said, gathering courage again, "it's stupid of you to insist on taking the blame for this. It was my fault, not yours. Can't you accept that?"

His eyes narrowed. "Are you by chance accusing me of having a guilt complex?" he asked, reading her with an ease that she found disconcerting.

"If you want me to make a diagnosis, Doctor," she said deliberately, "I'd have to answer yes to that."

It would have been easy to become frightened by the look on his face; his nostrils flared, his lips tightened, the aura of hate that she had first sensed about him seemed to brush her once again, but she refused to flinch from it.

He said coldly, "Knock off the doctor bit, will you? You know, I know, that I no longer deserve the title. Unless you're deliberately being sadistic in throwing it in my face. Perhaps you get your kicks from things like that. But I'd prefer you forget I ever had anything to do with medicine."

The aches and pains became submerged as sharp fury took over. "I do *not* get my kicks from being sadistic," she told him, her voice shaking. "Furthermore, you *are* a doctor, and you always will be one! It's not something you can deny. As for your guilt complex, I can't help it that you have one. It seems to me that you might practice some kind of—of psychoanalysis on yourself. I don't think you killed Chad in the first place! It seems to me the whole thing had to be an accident." The words were out before she had time to give them conscious thought, and there was no way of retracting them. "Anyway," she continued, this taking a lot more fortitude than she was sure she had, "you paid the price society asked of you. You're young, you've got a future, whether you believe in it or not. You've got to go on living!"

Silence made its own chasm, and Karen shivered at the depth of it. Then he said bitterly, "God, but I despise do-gooders!"

She thrust her chin upward. "I refuse to be labeled!"

"How can you possibly say you don't think I killed Chad?" he demanded. "What in hell can you possibly know about it?"

She could not look at him, and she wished, in fact, that Brad Simmons had been able to include in his prescriptions something that would have temporarily made her invisible!

Michael Stanhope, his words chipped from an ice block, said, "You should know from your own experiences that life isn't painted in pastel colors with a pot of gold at the end of every rainbow, but evidently you don't. No matter what happens, you try to go on living in your pretty little pink world. Well, it doesn't work that way, Karen Morse, with someone like me. I'm not interested in beautiful girls who get starry eyed at the thought of reforming ex-convicts like myself, and the world is overloaded with them, believe me. I'm not interested in *being* reformed, so you might as well get that through your head now, and save us both a lot of grief. Get out of my way after tonight, will you? I don't need you!"

She started to retort that she had never planned to get in his way in the first place, but the words never emerged. She began to tremble, in a kind of delayed reaction, and as the tears swam out of her eyes she dissolved into a crumpled little heap, sobbing her heart out while hating herself for this lamentable display of weakness in front of him.

Then she felt his arms around her; he was drawing her close to him, touching her eyes tenderly with something—another handkerchief? she wondered, and would have laughed except that, just now, there was no laughter in her. She felt his lips on her eyelids and, despite her aches, clung to him as they traveled to her mouth.

Karen stirred in response with an intensity that thoroughly surprised her, arching close to him, her breasts thrust against him, her arms twining around his neck, her fingers losing themselves in his thick pewter hair. Her mouth seemed to merge with his as his kiss deepened, sending in its wake a pure distillation of desire that seemed to become a part of the very blood flowing through her veins.

She did not want him to stop. Karen knew, with astonishing certainty, that she wanted those slender hands that had probed her so expertly in examination earlier today to explore her body in quite a different manner now. She wanted *him,* and when he released her it was close to unbearable to have him let her go, and she clung to him with all the strength she could summon only to have him set her aside, gently but firmly.

Michael started the car without a word, and as they left Burlington and Winooski behind them they became enmeshed in darkness and never ending rain, and the silence between them seemed to be interwoven with the night.

It occurred to her that during those three terrible years he had spent in prison, Michael Stanhope may well have become accustomed to silence, so that now he was more able than most people to repress speech.

Regardless, she wanted desperately to talk to him, to make *him* talk, but fatigue was taking over in shock's aftermath and she was coming to a temporary end of her physical rope.

She leaned her head back against the pillow; she dozed, only to come to wakefulness when the car turned off onto the side road that led to the two Stanhope homes, jolting despite Michael's skillful handling of it.

Seeing her stir, he said, "Sorry. Something should be done about these potholes but I suppose that's up to my father and Jerry."

Now, nearly at their journey's end, Karen yearned to be able to hold back time, if only briefly, because so much remained unsaid between them. But they had reached the fork in the road, Michael turned left, and around the bend they came upon the old farmhouse, blazing with lights.

Michael raised his eyebrows. "It would seem that you have a reception committee," he observed.

"Just Maida, I'm sure," Karen said. "She's probably worried about me."

But it wasn't just Maida. The kitchen door opened and Rod stood revealed, with Maida by his side.

With remarkable swiftness Rod came down the steps and across the ground that separated them, to open the door on Karen's side of the car and stare down at her anxiously.

"Damn you, Michael!" he said then, his voice thick with anger.

Before Karen could speak, Maida, just behind Rod, said to Michael, "Your father called. Did you really take Karen over to the hospital in Burlington?"

Michael's face was rigid, and for a moment Karen thought he was going to refuse to answer and almost started to answer for him. Then he said, "Why don't you phone and check? Ask for Dr. Bradley Simmons."

"Michael, you must understand!" Maida said. "We've all been frantic with worry."

"I understand perfectly," he said coldly.

Karen was about to speak, but Rod had begun to help her out of the car and she winced, despite herself, as she stood up.

Michael turned the ignition key and the engine roared to life as he said savagely, "Stand clear, will you? As you know, I'd be perfectly capable of running all of you down. In fact, it might almost be a pleasure!"

Chapter Six

Karen, shaken, looked after Michael Stanhope's rapidly receding car and said, "You're completely mistaken, Maida. Actually he probably saved my life. He braked immediately when he saw my headlights, or we would have crashed, and his car is a lot more substantial than the compact."

"That's what he *says,*" Maida pointed out with a cynicism that was unlike her.

"Are you sure about that?" Rod added skeptically.

"Sure that he stopped? Of course I am!"

"I would say," Rod observed judiciously, "that whatever happened, Michael was the cause of it. He drives like a madman. I followed him back from Burlington the other day—that is, I tried to. He was entirely too fast for me!"

"Maybe he has a death wish," Maida said.

Karen stared at her, appalled. "You're so *against* him!" she said finally.

"Why wouldn't we be against him?" Maida asked. "I don't know about Rod's reasoning, but Michael Stanhope has ruined my husband's life, among other things, which means that he's had quite an influence on my life, too."

Karen shook her head. "That's not true," she said, "and even if it were, you're wrong about this! The fault was entirely mine. I saw his car coming through the rain and I panicked."

She saw their disbelieving faces and said, "What is it you're thinking? Can you seriously believe that he was trying to harm *me*?"

"Hold it!" Rod said gently. "Let's all hold it, shall we, and get Karen inside where she can rest. You're right, Karen. Because it's Michael who was involved, we're overreacting."

"Thank you," Karen said, with more than a touch of cynicism.

Once inside, she sank gratefully onto the couch in the living room, and Rod mixed brandy and sodas with quick expertise. As he handed her glass to her he said, "Karen, try to understand. Michael has had a pretty traumatic effect on *all* our lives."

"What about *his* life?" she demanded.

Maida, whose cold was still at the miserable stage, sniffed audibly, then asked, "Why are you sticking up for him?"

Maida's beautiful face was definitely hostile, Karen saw to her surprise. At the moment, in fact, her favorite cousin seemed almost a stranger to her.

She said, trying to be low paced about it, "Look, I'm not sticking up for him. But I do wonder why you hate him so."

"*Hate*'s a strong word," Rod said, and she sensed that he too was trying to be low paced. "I don't think either Maida or I *hate* Michael, but I suppose it will be a long time before we'll be able to be objective about him. The fact of the matter tonight, though, is that Maida was worried about you, and so was I. I suppose it's natural in such a circumstance to try to find a scapegoat.''

"Michael is more than a scapegoat," Karen found herself saying. "It seems to me that he's a target."

Maida's face, she saw, was like a closed door. She said, "You should pause to think, Karen, that we've excellent reason for feeling about Michael as we do. You should stop to remember Chad for a moment."

Maida stood and said flatly, "I'm going to bed."

She left them and Rod, glancing at Karen's empty glass, asked, "Another brandy?"

"No, thank you," she said. "I've had medication; I'm not sure I should even have taken this one."

She added slowly, "I think I'll go to bed myself, if you'll excuse me, Rod. I'm feeling more than a bit battered."

"I can imagine," he sympathized ruefully. "I'll let myself out and lock the door behind me."

He stretched out a hand to help Karen up, but once she was standing he didn't at once release her fingers. He bent and kissed her lightly on the cheek and said, "Try to get some sleep. I'll check with you in the morning."

A moment later she heard the kitchen door close.

Despite her assorted aches Karen slept, a sleep entirely without dreams. She awakened to find that the rain was still falling. It was little more than a drizzle now but it would still not be a very good day to go fishing, she found herself thinking, remembering that it was Saturday. Ambrose, if not Michael himself, must be disappointed.

Michael. He had been a study in contrasts yesterday. She remembered his gentleness as he cared for her in his father's house, his verbal brutality on the ride to Burlington, and later, in the restaurant parking lot. But there had also been a glimpse of humor and one marvelously revealing smile when at the hospital he had teased Brad Simmons.

Most vivid of all were the memories of those moments when he had held her in a way that made his arms seem a sanctuary, his kiss arousing her to an intensity she still found hard to credit.

As she lay in bed, watching the raindrops trace descending patterns on the windowpanes, Karen felt herself stirred in a way that had been entirely outside her experience for a long, long while. In fact, she admitted to herself, no one had *ever* stirred her as quickly and thoroughly as Michael Stanhope had done, and she knew only too well that this was something that must be shut off now. Any other course could only lead to danger.

Danger. It was not physical danger that she was thinking of, for despite Maida, despite Rod, despite anyone, she knew instinctively that she had nothing at all to fear in that respect from Michael. Rather, it was the danger of risking her love upon a man who would only toss it back in her face.

Love. How quickly she had let the word creep into her vocabulary where this distant, enigmatic, gray-haired stranger was concerned! She tried to tell herself that she was not defining her emotions correctly, that it was a surface attraction only, that the feelings he had evoked in her yesterday had been a purely physical reaction in the aftermath of trauma. And she knew, ruefully, that she was only fooling herself!

She got out of bed, finding that Brad Simmons had been right in his prediction. She did ache, but her right arm wasn't suffering any more than the rest of her, which surely proved that it was getting stronger.

Maida, she ascertained, was still asleep, so she went out to the kitchen and brewed a pot of coffee. She took a cup of it into the living room and stood at the window looking out over a lake that was very much the same color as Michael Stanhope's hair. The sky was a pale gray blanket, obscuring sight, and the distant Adirondacks had disappeared from view.

She wished that Michael and Ambrose would come walking along the lakefront, despite the rain, and with that wish came the knowledge of how much she wanted to see him again.

The phone rang, and Karen quickly made her way into the kitchen to answer it, hoping it wouldn't awaken Maida.

It was Rod. "I forgot to tell you last night that I've got a long-standing dinner date in Albany this weekend," he told her. "I should be back by late tomorrow afternoon, and I won't go at all, for that matter, if you need me."

"Rod," she said, "you've no need at all to cancel any plans or rush back here because of yesterday, if that's what you're thinking about."

"I admit I don't relish having you here by yourself with Michael Stanhope loose."

"That's a dreadful way to put it," she told him tightly.

"I suppose it is," he conceded. "Regardless, be a bit on the careful side, will you?"

"Yes," she said.

The phone call had awakened Maida. She came out of her room a few minutes later, still heavy-eyed and somewhat stuffy, but insisting, nevertheless, that her cold was definitely on the mend.

"What about you?" she asked, surveying Karen narrowly. "I'm surprised that you're even able to move this morning."

Karen smiled. "I'm tougher than I look!"

They settled down with cups of coffee. The signposts pointed to a talk about last night, but for the moment Karen wanted to leave this subject alone. She professed an interest in the mystery novel she was reading and hoped that Maida, supposedly immersed in a book of her own, wouldn't notice that every now and then she became so lost in thought she forgot to turn the pages.

They had lunch, they took naps, and in the midafternoon the phone rang again. This time, they both headed for the kitchen to answer it. *Boredom,* Karen thought, *or we wouldn't be so anxious!*

Maida picked up the receiver first. As Karen watched, Maida registered surprise, dismay, and uncertainty, in quick order. These were all trained reactions, for Maida could simulate almost any emotion and be totally convincing about it. *But she's not on stage now,* Karen thought.

Then Maida cupped her hand over the mouthpiece and said softly, "It's Uncle Doug. He wants us both to come over for a drink."

She sniffed, as if testing out the veracity of her cold as a possible excuse, but before she could translate action into words Karen said quickly, "Let's."

There was nothing at all theatrical about Maida's

expression now. She was genuinely astonished. She said hesitantly, "Uncle Doug? My cousin says she'd like very much to meet you. Five? We'll be there."

She hung up the receiver, then looked across at Karen, annoyed. "Now, why did I let you talk me into that?" she demanded.

"Maybe," Karen suggested, "because you want to go and see him yourself."

Maida shook her head. "No, I don't." She paused. "On the other hand," she deliberated, "perhaps I do. I don't know. I have no desire to become involved with any of Jerry's family under the circumstances. I don't want to have to make a lot of explanations."

As they went back into the living room Maida said slowly, "I suppose I sound horribly selfish. Uncle Doug is a very dear person, and I admire him tremendously. It's just that I don't want any part of the Stanhopes right now. Last night, when he called to tell me about your accident, he sounded so much like Jerry that for a moment I thought it *was* Jerry."

It was a revealing statement. Karen found herself thinking, *you still* do *love Jerry!* She almost spoke aloud, catching herself just in time. This wasn't the moment to go into it.

Karen had brought very few clothes with her and this, of course, was not a dress-up occasion. Yet she found herself selecting a pale gold dress with an unusually becoming scooped neckline, and added a topaz pendant, which emphasized the color of the dress while at the same time it seemed to deepen the amber tone of her eyes.

She paid careful attention to her makeup and

brushed her ash-blond hair until it gleamed. She even used a daub of her favorite L'Air du Temps perfume, then, checking her appearance in the mirror, was thankful that none of her bruises were where they could be seen.

She again borrowed a raincoat and rainhat from Maida, then followed Maida's lead through a narrow path through the spruces that wound around Rod's cottage, ending at the judge's driveway.

Now it was Maida who let the heavy brass door knocker rise and fall. Horace, answering its summons, was polite but taciturn.

The front door opened into a rectangular foyer. Directly ahead, a long living room overlooked the lake. Muted colors and exquisite antique furnishings merged to register a memory at once vague and distinct, paradoxical though that might seem, and Karen realized that this must be the room into which she had been taken after yesterday's accident.

Horace led them through the living room and down a corridor that culminated in a large circular library, formed by one of the turrets that punctuated either end of the house. There were windows around half the room, yielding incredible views of the lake in three directions. The rest of the wall space was lined with bookcases. A fireplace was alive with blazing logs, spiral tongues of gold and apricot licking the well-used bricks. There were big leather chairs, lamps, tables, memorabilia, a *world*. A man could live with the changing seasons in this room, Karen mused, almost becoming a part of each of them, reveling in their special glories without ever having to go outdoors.

The judge was a genial host. As Karen and Maida settled, at his suggestion, into chairs that faced the fireplace, he maneuvered his wheelchair, placing himself between them.

Karen, trying not to be obvious about it as she observed him, could not help but feel a pang of pity for him. She remembered how yesterday, even in her dazed condition, she had sensed the power and vitality still latent in him, even though she knew that he was confined to the wheelchair, unable to walk at all.

He smiled across at her, and she had the uncomfortable feeling that he knew what she was thinking. He said, "I was relieved when Michael came back last night and told me your injuries were not serious." There was a roguishness about him as he added, "You *look* wonderful. How do you feel?"

"A bit battered," Karen said lightly, "but not too bad, considering."

"Good for you! And you, Maida? You sounded miserable yesterday. Your cold seems better."

"It is, thank you."

"I forgot to ask you how Jerry is," the judge continued.

"He's fine," Maida hedged.

"Does he plan to join you shortly?"

Maida hesitated. "No," she said. "That is, I don't think so. He's quite busy just now."

Horace brought a tray with an assortment of drinks and hors d'oeuvres, and Karen knew that her cousin was relieved by this interruption. Maida clearly had no desire as yet to confess to her uncle-in-law that she and her husband were on the verge of a divorce.

As they chatted casually about a number of things,

Karen found herself waiting for Michael to join them, then finally realized that there was a strong possibility he was not going to do so at all. She wished that there were some way to bring him into the conversation, yet there was no easy chance to manage this.

At length, she commented on the beauty of the view beyond the windows and the judge said, with the only touch of sadness he had permitted himself thus far, "I live with it. Perhaps, sometimes, *for* it." He laughed, quickly changing the mood. "That doesn't make me very busy, does it?" he asked, then answered his own question. "I am, however. I've a number of projects lined up. One of these days, I may write a book. In the meantime I'm cataloging my late wife's mineral collection. It is an extensive one, for we traveled a great deal over the years, often in connection with her work, and amassed specimens from all sorts of places. When the collection has been put together properly it is to go to the museum in New York with which she was affiliated when I met her. That was her wish. It's quite a job to get it together, though. Scientists, I find, are inclined to be messy, and my Eleanor was a true scientist!"

He spoke of his late wife with affection and humor, and this touched Karen. She said softly, "My father was a geologist. He always promised to take me on some of his field trips to faraway places, but he died when I was still in high school. There was never time."

"Perhaps," the judge suggested, "you'd like to see Eleanor's collection one of these days, when you've a free moment?"

"I should love to," Karen told him sincerely.

"Then come along, whenever you have the chance. There is another circular room at the opposite end of the house that I've set up as a workshop. I'm afraid you'll find it a total disaster, but I *am* making progress, even though it's slow. If either Horace or I could type, it would help! If I had my way, I'd make typing a required subject for every schoolchild."

This led into the subject of education in general, and on to other things, none of which verged on the personal.

Horace brought a second round of drinks and, as they were finishing them, Karen realized that the rain had stopped, and now there were shadows lengthening across the lake, pearl merging to charcoal, which, in time, would merge to indigo.

Maida, glancing at her watch, said, "I'd no idea it was so late! We must go!"

Karen surprised an expression on the judge's face that gave her the strong impression that he too was waiting for something, or, rather, for someone. But Michael, she was certain now, was not about to appear.

Reluctantly the judge followed them into the living room, handling his wheelchair with practiced dexterity. It was then that Karen saw the grand piano in the far corner, and inadvertently she whispered, "Oh!"

It was a small moan, but the judge heard it and turned to her swiftly. He followed her gaze and said, "Would you like to try it? It's probably hopelessly out of tune, but even so...."

Karen shook her head. "No," she said stiffly. "I no longer play."

"Have you tried?" the judge asked softly.

It was a question that might well have angered her, had it come from anyone else, but this man, she knew, had also suffered more than his share.

"No," she said, her voice very low.

"If you would ever care to do so, you're more than welcome."

Karen smiled wistfully. "The mineral collection, yes," she told him. "But the piano...I don't think so."

As the door closed behind them, she thought about this and was surprised because she hadn't flatly said no.

Maida had had the foresight to bring a flashlight, and she switched it on as they made their way toward the path that led through the woods. Karen noticed, as they crossed the driveway, that there was a three-car garage to one side. Two of the doors were closed, but the third one stood open, revealing Michael's orange car.

This confirmed her feeling that he had been here all the while, studiously avoiding them. She wondered if even now he might be standing at a window in the growing darkness, watching them depart.

Chapter Seven

The rain had washed the sky, rinsed the trees, cleansed even the surface of the lake, so that on Sunday morning the whole world stood revealed in bright new colors. Karen awoke, knowing that she had dreamed, but the dream had not been a nightmare. Had it been all *that* easy to exorcise her own ghosts?

She heard a strange pinging sound that came from the direction of the window on her left. An animal of some sort? she wondered. Then the noise came again, and this time she was watching and saw something hit the glass and bounce off.

Her heart thudding, she got out of bed and crept across the floor, trying to be noiseless, peeking, then nearly gasping with relief. Ambrose stood beneath her window, his arm raised, about to throw yet another pebble. She forestalled him by standing up very suddenly, and he stopped, his fist in midair.

She fumbled with the latch on the window and pushed it open, this entailing some effort and forcing her right arm to do some of the work.

"Ambrose," she hissed.

"Shush," he said, his freckled face wrinkled into a scowl. "You'll wake up your cousin."

She glanced at her wristwatch. She said, "Do you know that it's only seven o'clock?"

"That's late for fishing," he said sturdily.

"What do you mean?"

"Couldn't go yesterday," Ambrose pointed out logically. "Not with that kind of rain. Don't mind fishing in a drizzle, but not in that downpour." He sounded at least forty.

"So?" she asked.

"So, we're going this morning," said Ambrose, obviously restraining his impatience. "If you'll hurry up and get ready so as we don't have to wait till noon to get started."

"*I* hurry up?"

Ambrose grinned. It was a beautiful grin. He said, "You can come with us."

In his opinion he was conveying the ultimate favor on her, and at the moment she was inclined to agree with him. Somehow, Michael had given permission—which meant that despite his failure to appear for cocktails last night he must not be all that averse to seeing her again.

She suddenly felt surprisingly carefree and the smile she turned on Ambrose was radiant. "Give me five minutes," she said. Then, as she turned away, a thought struck her. She stuck her head out the window and whistled softly, and Ambrose reappeared around the side of the house.

"Ambrose," she said, "if you're taking a picnic with you I haven't got any food to bring."

"That's okay," Ambrose said generously. "Mom made enough for all of us."

Karen snatched the pair of jeans she'd brought along, donned a sweater, and also borrowed Maida's heavy coat again. She brushed her hair and tied it back with a ribbon, put on her sneakers, and paused to write a rather ambiguous note for Maida that would, at least, keep her from worrying. Then she dashed out of the house, thankful that Maida was both a sound sleeper and a late sleeper.

She went quickly to the rickety flight of steps that led down to the lakefront, negotiated them, and saw Michael and Ambrose and the boat just to her left. Michael was wearing a gray wool shirt and faded old jeans, and there was no welcome at all in his face as he looked across at her.

In a terrible, sinking moment she realized that the invitation had been purely Ambrose's idea. Well, Ambrose's intentions were good, she was sure of that. And it was flattering to think that a boy his age wanted her to join what, she knew, must be a very private sort of party. Ambrose adored Michael, that was evident every time he looked at him. So these occasions when they went off on a man-to-man basis certainly must mean a great deal to him.

On the other hand Michael didn't seem surprised, so perhaps Ambrose had told him after all that he'd gone and waked her up and had been pretty insistent about her coming along. She hoped so! She'd never been one to intrude, she wouldn't have come at all— even though she could imagine that Ambrose might have gotten pretty vocal in his protests if she had out-right refused—but it had seemed to her that she and Michael had begun to step forth on a very different footing after her accident the other night. His kiss, even though he had wrenched himself away after-ward, had been indication enough of that. And he had spoken to her of a number of things that she doubted he'd spoken to anyone else about. With bitterness—true, with antagonism—he had even seemed to be trying at moments to provoke a negative reaction in her. Yet the whole thing had marked progress. Or, so she had thought.

Now she wasn't at all sure. It occurred to her that maybe Michael would just as soon forget about the other night and retreat back into his own shell. And that was what it was. An invisible shell, a very tough shell. He'd covered every inch of himself with it.

Standing there, looking up into a face that was singularly blank, she would have given a great deal to know what he really was thinking. But he offered her no clue.

Her earlier sense of joy changed to despondency, and she said, "Look, I really don't have to come, you know. If—"

Almost simultaneously, he began, "Look, you really don't have to go if you don't want to—"

They broke off at close to the same instant, then glanced as if by one accord at Ambrose, who was busy stashing things into the boat and, just now, was out of hearing range.

Michael's smile was wry as he said, "It was Ambrose's idea, I admit, but that doesn't mean you have to go along with it. I didn't know he was going to wake you, or I would have stopped him. I'd say that after the things that have been happening to you recently you need to get all the rest you can."

It was a rather oblique statement, and she decided to disregard it. This time, it was she who forced their eyes to meet, and it seemed to her that something flickered in his, something specific enough to give her courage. She became very sure that Michael Stanhope wasn't nearly as emotionless as he tried to have people think he was—nor, for that matter, nearly so angry, nor so hostile.

She said, "If you have no objection, I'd really like to come. It's a long time since I've done anything like this. Not since I was a little girl and my father and I used to go fishing together."

Michael nodded. "Come along, then."

There was no particular encouragement to the way he said it, no especial warmth, but she was not about to quibble. She trailed behind him down to the water-front, then followed instructions about getting into the boat. She let herself be pushed in it out into the water, at which point first Ambrose clambered aboard, and then Michael.

Michael rowed, and Ambrose, trailing his fingers in the water, said, "Still mighty cold." Karen remembered his father telling her how Ambrose had fallen through the ice, how Michael had rescued him. Yet there seemed no trace of fright in Ambrose about water, cold or otherwise. *You're a better doctor than you think, Michael Stanhope.*

She looked up to meet his eyes; they were so intent upon her that he flushed, slightly, and quickly looked away.

"Like it?" Ambrose inquired.

"It's beautiful," she told him.

He grinned and said, "See, Mike. I told you she would." But Michael didn't answer.

They followed the contour of the island, just as they had the other day when she'd been watching them from Maida's window, going around to the other side so that Grand Isle was blotted from view and Lake Champlain's western expanse stretched out before them. Michael rounded a promontory with sheer, rocky sides topped by dark, pointed firs. All at once they were in a cove, an oasis of such quiet beauty that she gasped.

There was a half-moon of surprisingly white sand, and Michael made for it. They beached the boat, and Ambrose asked, "Want me to take the tackle on up?"

"Yes," Michael said. "I think we'll pause for a cup of coffee first."

Ambrose scampered across the beach, carrying fishing rods and a bait box, and seemed almost at once to be swallowed up by the thick growth of the conifers. Michael produced a thermos bottle, filled two plastic cups with steaming coffee, and handed one to her. She started instinctively to reach for it with her right hand, then switched, took it with her left, and he frowned slightly.

"You should try," he said. "You've got to build up confidence."

"And suppose I drop the whole thing?" she countered.

"You're going to have to take some chances or you'll never get the strength back into it," he said. And then, at the expression on her face, "Okay. Don't say it."

"But I'm going to say it," she told him. "Why don't *you* take some chances? Where *were* you last night?"

"In my room," he admitted. "I was trying to read."

"And when we left—were you watching us?"

"Yes."

"I could feel your eyes on my back," she said. "I hate feeling anyone's eyes on my back. Even yours."

Even yours. If he caught the significance of her remark he let it go by without comment. He said, "Look, it was kind of you to accept my father's invitation last night. He doesn't have many visitors. Principally because of me." This was said without inflection. "I— well, I'm not very good in the so-called social situations anymore and he knows it. So he spares me, which isn't right either. I mean, he deserves to have people around; he likes people."

"And you don't?"

"You're damned right I don't," he said with a savagery that startled her. But then he quickly added, "Look, to get back to you last night—it did Dad good to have you and Maida come over, you especially. He said you're going to come and see my mother's mineral collection one of these days, and I hope you will."

"I intend to," she said, "but to go back to last night again—is that why you didn't join us, because you don't like people?"

"Maida wouldn't have wanted me there," he said.

"Are you sure of that?"

"Of course I am," he said impatiently. "Just looking at me brings back too many painful memories. Not just of Chad. Of my mother too. Maida was very fond of my mother." And, as he saw her puzzled expression, "Didn't you know? I killed her too."

Ambrose chose entirely the wrong moment to reappear. He emerged from the edge of the woods to cup his hands and shout, "Hey, you two! Are you going to come and do some fishing?"

Karen tried to disregard him, even though she knew this would be close to impossible for very long. Like most kids his age, Ambrose would be persistent, she was sure, and right now there was no doubt at all that he wanted to get their expedition going. But she didn't feel that she could start out with this last statement of Michael's hanging between them.

"Michael," she began, but he shook his head.

"I didn't intend to shock you," he said quietly. "I was sure that Maida and Rod had filled you in on everything negative they could about me. Karen," he said as she started to protest, "we can't very well get into it now. Some other time, maybe...."

The words trailed off as he surveyed her thoughtfully. Then he asked, almost as if she weren't there, "What is it about you? I don't talk about things like this to...anyone." That heart-tugging crooked smile came to twist his lips. "What kind of a sorceress are you?" he asked, almost lightly, and then added, "Come on. Ambrose isn't known for his patience."

She gave him her empty coffee cup and clambered out of the boat. At once Ambrose shouted, "Follow me," and she did, along a path that led through the woods and then veered uphill until they came to a clearing, which, she saw, was in reality a large expanse of rocky ledges thrust out over the lake. The ledges were laced with miniature chasms. Karen peered down into one and, far below, saw water swirling.

They fished, using handlines baited with worms, dangling them down through the rocks until they reached deep into the water. And they were rewarded. By midmorning they had a catch of perch, plus a few rock bass.

Ambrose said wistfully, "Mike, I wish you'd build a fire so we could clean them and cook them right out here. That's how they taste best, you know that."

Michael nodded. "Maybe so," he admitted. "But this time you take them home and give them to your folks, and your mother can cook them for Sunday night supper."

"Would you and Karen come eat with us?" By this time "Mrs. Morse" had gone by the boards with Ambrose.

"Not tonight," said Michael. "Your mother fixed our lunch, Ambrose. She deserves a break."

"Then let's eat some of the lunch she fixed," said Ambrose practically, and Karen agreed.

At first she had been oppressed by her conversation with Michael, it was as if there were a black cloud hanging over them. But with Ambrose for company, with the excitement of catching the fish, the cloud had lifted. Michael responded to Ambrose, they teased each other, and occasionally Michael smiled his rare smile. Once or twice he laughed at something Ambrose said in a way that was almost lighthearted. It became a good time for all three of them.

Now Karen was hungry; she was as enthusiastic as Ambrose when it came to attacking his mother's excellent sandwiches and hermit cookies. The sun touched the rocky ledges to warmth; Michael had brought an old blanket and Karen stretched out on it, and promptly fell asleep.

She awakened to silence, and thought momentarily

that both Michael and Ambrose had abandoned her.
But Michael was sitting nearby, smoking a pipe, his
eyes fixed on something that, she suspected, was far
more distant than the horizon.

He looked across at her and smiled, and her heart
lurched. He said, "There's some coffee left. Want
some?"

"Please."

He divided the contents, held a cup out to her. But
when she reached for it with her left hand he shook
his head. "No. Use your right one," he insisted.

"But suppose—"

"Try," he interrupted.

She closed her fingers around the cup, held it,
drank from it. She said, "It's wobbly, but it's working."

"You have to give anything a chance," he said.
And this time he didn't have to add the admonition,
"Don't say it." She was not about to retaliate or to get
into areas with him that were either painful or contro-
versial. Not just now.

"Where's Ambrose?" she asked.

"Exploring," said Michael. "I think he's certain
that this island is still inhabited by Indians, and that
one of these days he's going to come face to face with
one of them."

Karen, feeling her way, said, "His father told me
that you—well, that you saved Ambrose's life last
winter."

"Roger?" Michael's eyebrows raised in surprise.
"When did you manage a talk with Roger Barnes?"

"Friday," she said. "I'd gone up to the store to get
some aspirin and fruit juice for Maida."

"Yes," he said, "I know." He tapped the tobacco dregs out of his pipe. "Roger gives me credit for more than I did."

"I doubt that," she said. "You underestimate yourself."

He looked across at her quizzically. "Trying to play psychiatrist?" he asked.

She could feel herself flushing. "I'm not sure I know what you mean," she hedged.

"If you're trying to figure out what makes me tick, save your time," he told her roughly. "I had more than my share of the head doctors in prison! I was evaluated and evaluated again and then reevaluated. I've no intention of becoming anyone's subject again, whether they are motivated by a curiosity that is professional or, like yours, entirely idle."

She felt as if he had slapped her, his rejection was so swift and total that she flinched visibly, and to her thorough annoyance she could feel betraying tears start into her eyes.

"Not that again!" Michael said, his tone tinged with disgust. "Aren't you afraid I'll run out of handkerchiefs?"

She could not possibly have answered him, much as she would have loved to fling a scathing retort right in his teeth. She got to her feet, turning away, thinking only of escape; but she was so blinded by her tears that at once she stumbled.

He covered the space between them with incredible speed. She felt his arms around her, drawing her back, and blinking, she saw that she had come right to the edge of one of the mini chasms.

"Don't you have any sense at all?" Michael shouted

angrily. "You could have sprained an ankle, at the least! What do you want, Karen? This?"

Before she could twist out of his arms, his grip tightened, clamping her shoulders with a force that hurt. His mouth descended with equal force, his lips bruising, demanding.

She was ashamed at the brevity of her struggle, but she could not deny her response to him. His hands dropped to her waist, and he pushed up the fabric of her T-shirt, those long fingers, exploring, arousing feelings so sensuous that they were, in themselves, flagrant danger signals, and yet she let him go on.

Then, even as she was arching herself toward him, fitting the curve of her body against his own male hardness, he let go of her so abruptly that she staggered and would have fallen if he hadn't caught her arm again.

"You've been married," he said bitterly. "I suppose that gives you some excuse, but not enough. Am I to assume that you're merely sex-starved, or that you think it would be a different kind of thrill to make it with an ex-convict?"

She stared at him, horrified, and he laughed, but it was a short, unpleasant laugh. "Don't look so shocked," he told her. "Don't you think I know I'm a curiosity to you? I'm a freak to everyone I meet!"

He turned away from her, but she was past compassion for him. She felt a sudden surge of pure fury, and she said, seething, "Is that what you really think, Michael? Do you *really* think I feel as if you're something out of a human zoo?"

The terrible silence that followed seemed interminable, and then he asked, a ragged edge to his voice that she would never forget, "Don't you?"

She was unable to answer because Ambrose again chose an entirely wrong moment to reappear. He came skipping across the ledges, shouting, "Hey, look, you guys! I've found something I'm going to give the judge for his collection!"

He held out an object that shone in the sunlight. "I think maybe I've found a gold mine!"

Michael looked down at the glittering chunk and said, "It's pyrite. Fool's gold." His eyes met Karen's, and she winced at the bleak expression in them. "Appropriate, isn't it?" he asked her.

Although Ambrose definitely was not ready to leave the island, Michael convinced him that if the fish they had caught were to be delivered fresh they would have to get under way.

Even Ambrose was quiet on the row back, and as they touched shore he climbed out of the boat, then helped Michael drag it to high ground. It was Michael, however, who helped Karen out, and there was a gravity to his features that reminded her of an expression she had often seen on Hugh MacKnight's face immediately after an important medical consultation.

"Better get on home with those fish, Ambrose," Michael said.

Ambrose nodded. "Sure you don't want some, Karen?" he offered.

"Not this time, thanks, Ambrose," she told him. She stretched the truth. "I'm sure my cousin already has something planned for dinner."

Ambrose took off along the lakefront path. Evidently, Karen assumed, he had his own shortcut back to the store and his adjacent house.

Left alone with Michael, Karen sought an escape route of her own, for that final encounter between them on the island had wearied her to the point of defeat.

She said, almost formally, "Thank you for taking me today."

Michael looked down at her, his mouth taut. She saw his jaw twitch and she thought, *He's holding it in. He's holding everything in!*

He said, his voice low, "I'm sorry I spoiled it for you. I'm especially sorry for the way I behaved and the things I said to you there on the island. I don't know how I can possibly—"

The sentence was left unfinished. They heard someone calling their names and looked up to see Rod Kensington standing atop the bluff above them.

"I'm back," he said, unnecessarily.

Now a woman appeared at his side, slim and with Rod's same bright yellow hair. She was a seductive and captivating figure in vivid purple slacks, topped by a blouse bright with swirling colors.

"Well, *hello,*" she said, and Karen saw that she was looking directly at Michael.

She could feel him start, but he said coolly enough, "Hello, June. Karen, this is Rod's twin sister."

June Kensington. She too had been at Chad Stanhope's apartment on that terrible, tragic night!

"June met me in Albany," Rod called down to them, "and I persuaded her to come back for a visit. Maida's asked us over for a drink. Come on and join us."

The invitation of necessity included Michael, Karen realized, and June Kensington underlined this. "You too, Michael," she said, as if to make sure that there was no doubt about it.

Karen actually could see Michael tense, but he only nodded and followed her up the steps and on into the farmhouse. Maida, putting a tape on the stereo, greeted them with a wave, and Rod took orders for drinks.

As music flooded the room June said, "Turn it down a little, will you, Maida, so we can hear ourselves talk? How are you, Michael?"

There was a quality to the question, a certain depth of concern, that made a new awareness wash over Karen. She realized suddenly that June Kensington was not *really* Michael's cousin, not by blood, for now she remembered that Maida had told her Michael was adopted. No, there was an entirely different kind of relationship between them, a kind of common denomination.

She became increasingly convinced of this as June dominated the conversation, seemingly oblivious of the tension around them, and there *was* tension.

Rod seemed determined to be a good host, yet Karen noted that not once did he speak to Michael directly. Maida too, though pleasant on the surface, was avoiding any direct conversation with Michael, while June, Karen thought ironically, seemed to be playing the part of a flame engaged in trying to lure a moth within its aura.

Michael, irritatingly enough, did not seem to mind her perching on the arm of the chair he was sitting in, even though his answers to her ceaseless and not quite audible questions were evidently monosyllabic.

After a time Karen had had enough of it, and she said, "Why don't I get some cheese and crackers, Maida?"

Maida, who was going over a selection of stereo tapes with Rod, absently said, "Fine."

As she started toward the kitchen Karen was surprised when June Kensington said quickly, "I'll help you."

There was no gracious way of refusing, and as it was, her bad arm seemed determined to resist doing her bidding. She fumbled at the task of assembling a tray of assorted cheese, some pâté, Melba Toast rounds, wheat crackers, and she nearly cut herself opening a tin of salted nuts.

To her chagrin, June swiftly came to her rescue, managing to put everything together with irritating efficiency.

As she did so Rod's twin sister said, "Michael has *aged* so! I still can't quite believe that gray hair." It was a seemingly casual comment, but then she continued, more carefully, "How is he doing, do you think?"

Karen too chose the careful route. "I don't know him well enough to make a comparison," she said. "We met for the first time only a few days ago."

Was it her imagination, she wondered, or did June seem relieved by this? She frowned as they went back into the living room, June carrying the laden tray, which she placed on a coffee table in front of the couch.

Perversely Karen took a platter of cheese and crackers across to Michael, forcing herself to use her right hand as she passed it to him, while praying that the hand would not fail her. He noticed and said very softly, "Keep it up," and for a moment his green eyes seemed to come alive as he looked up at her. Inadvertently she glanced at June and was at once aware that June, though unaware of the reason for this byplay, had noticed it.

Michael finished his drink and stood. "I have to be getting along," he said. "Dad's expecting me."

Maida and Rod said good-bye, as briefly as possible, while June told him brightly, that she'd be over to see the judge in the morning.

He nodded at this, without making comment, his eyes swinging to Karen, and they were riveting in their intensity. She knew suddenly that she simply couldn't let him leave without going back to the conversation on the lakefront that had been interrupted by Rod. She must tell him that he had not ruined her day, that, in fact, this was a day she would forever remember!

As he stood on the threshold she said quickly, "Michael!"

He raised his eyebrows. "Yes?"

"I'm afraid I left my sunglasses in the boat," she said, stumbling over the words. "I wonder, would you mind taking a look with me?"

"Not at all," he said coolly and waited for her to join him.

Her pulse was thumping as they walked across the grass to the steps, and at the top he said, "We'd better go down one at a time. Jerry should do something about these before someone takes a real tumble."

He went first, turning back to catch her hand as she negotiated the last two rickety steps. The mere touch of his fingers was so arousing that she trembled, but he let go almost immediately, leaving her with a sense of incredulity at the reaction he provoked in her without even trying to do so.

As they neared the boat she said hesitantly, "The sunglasses aren't there."

He looked down at her quizzically. "What do you mean?"

"I didn't leave them behind," she confessed. "I wanted an excuse to talk to you alone for a moment, that's all."

"Oh?"

There was no encouragement in his voice, and his face was expressionless. Karen said tentatively, "I wanted to tell you that I...enjoyed the day very much."

A smile brushed across his face, but it was a purely sardonic smile, and there was a definite skepticism this time in his "Oh?"

"You had said," she reminded him, "that you were afraid you spoiled the day for me."

"I had?" he queried infuriatingly. Then, administering a clearcut verbal slap, he added, "I'm sorry, Karen. I'd forgotten."

Chapter Eight

As Karen walked into the living room again to face Maida, Rod and June, she wished desperately that the family distribution of acting ability had been more equal; just now she could have done with a measure of Maida's share of it.

Rod, glancing up, asked, "Did you find your sunglasses?"

"No," she said, "I must have left them out on the island."

That was that; the conversation switched to other things, and eventually Rod and June went back to their cottage.

Michael's cool rebuff still smarted. She knew that he hadn't "forgotten" anything that had gone between them any more than she had. So why, then, had he feigned such indifference when she'd deliberately made a chance to be alone with him, so that they'd have the opportunity to speak in private, if only briefly?

There had been an intensity in each of their encounters unlike anything she had ever experienced before. They had run a gamut of emotions, and she had the nagging certainty that the truest of them had been in those moments when she had been in his arms, his kisses evoking an entirely new depth of feeling in her.

She felt now as if she had been dormant for a long, long time and Michael had awakened her. A Sleeping Beauty? She asked herself this whimsically and then could not help but be amused by the thought that if this were the case Michael would automatically be cast in the role of Prince Charming. And she could not imagine his agreeing to play it.

Karen sobered. He had his share of hang-ups, that was certain. But then so did she. Or, at least, she had. She amended the tense because, miraculously, the things that had been the worst, traumatically speaking, suddenly seemed to have had their edges dulled. Her own past had faded, there was a blur to memory. Thinking about this, she began to believe that old adage that time healed. . . . Something that she had seriously doubted all those months when she was in the process of recuperating from emotional as well as physical injuries.

Would time ever blur memory for Michael? Would the edges of his pain ever be softened? She knew only too well that she'd like to have a hand in the process of accomplishing this, but at the very thought she shied away. It was one thing to become "involved," as Hugh MacKnight had suggested, but quite another thing to deliberately dive into a whirling sea of unknown depth!

Also, there was no doubt at all that Michael had been willing enough to accept June Kensington's invitation to stop for a drink, and they had chatted together in a fashion that had been close to intimate. Karen found herself stiffening at the thought of this, and then, to her astonishment, recognized the pang that stabbed her for what it was. Jealousy!

She told herself quickly that she had no reason to be jealous over Michael Stanhope. It was a slight dent to her pride to think that he'd turned away from her and to June so swiftly—though she had to admit, on contemplating this, that it hadn't been quite that way. The rebuff down on the waterfront may have had nothing to do with June's arrival on the scene. It may simply have been a matter of letting her know that he didn't want to prolong this newfound association.

Well, she told herself defiantly, neither did she!

She glanced at the clock and saw that it was nearly eight, then realized that there was a chance Hugh MacKnight might be expecting her in the office tomorrow morning. At the least she should have called him before now to tell him that she couldn't make it before Tuesday, and even this would mean rushing things.

On the other hand there was certainly no reason to linger on Grand Isle any longer. By now Maida must have gotten over her initial fear of Michael. It was understandable that he'd frightened her that first night, prowling around in the dark with a flashlight and actually coming into her room. On the other hand it was foolish of Maida not to have taken him to account about this before now. Karen felt that there must be a simple explanation. Very possibly Jerry had asked Michael to keep a watch on the house.

Even if this were not the case, she could not believe that Maida had anything to fear from Michael. Further, Rod and June were little more than a stone's throw away, and the judge was right at the other end of the phone. Then, there was also Horace to be relied upon. Maida could hardly be safer.

Thinking of the judge, Karen frowned. She wished she had managed a visit with him by herself, for she had felt a special affinity for him and would really have liked to see his wife's mineral collection. There would not be time for it now, though. First thing in the morning, she decided, she must drive to the Burlington Airport. The rental-car people had come out the day after her accident to tow away the first car and replace it with a bright green substitute. Now she would turn back the second car and see if there was anything that needed to be done about the first one, and then catch the next plane that would take her to New York.

Maida was in the kitchen, putting away the remnants of the hors d'oeuvres, and now Karen sought her out to ask her if she'd mind her phoning Hugh MacKnight. Although she disliked the prospect of calling Hugh at home because of the chance of having his wife, Sara, answer the phone and become unpleasant about it, there seemed no alternative just now.

"He may be expecting me in the morning," she explained to Maida. "But obviously I can't make it till Tuesday."

Maida's consternation was dismaying. "You can't go!" she wailed.

"Oh, come, Maida," Karen said, smiling, trying to keep it light. "Surely you realize by now that there is nothing to be afraid of where Michael Stanhope is concerned. There has to be a logical explanation for his having come into the house that first night you were here, and I think you should ask him about it.''

"All right," Maida said, "I pushed the panic button, I admit it. Nevertheless, this has been a very bad time for me, and it helps tremendously to have you here. But the problem is that I need to go away myself for a couple of days. I have an appointment with my lawyer in Boston tomorrow."

"Oh?"

"Don't look like that, Karen. I really must talk to him. There are so many things that must be gone over," Maida continued, looking acutely unhappy as she spoke. "And I hate to close the house up for the brief time I'll be gone."

"Couldn't Rod and June Kensington—or Michael, for that matter—keep an eye on it for you?"

"Possibly, but I wouldn't feel right about it. It isn't my house, after all. I would feel terrible if there were a fire, for instance, or vandalism. I'd never forgive myself."

Maida, Karen sensed, was hedging, and now her lovely cousin shrugged and said, "The fact of the matter is that I can't bear to come back here and find the place empty. I'll be grateful forever," she added dramatically, "if you'll stay on just a few days longer."

Just a few days longer! Maida, Karen thought wryly, had no idea what she was asking. To linger on Grand Isle would mean almost certainly seeing Michael again, and exposing herself to the sting of his indifference. Also, if he and June Kensington were on the verge of taking up wherever it was they had left off, it would be pure torment to see them together.

There was no point in deliberately steering a course that would only make her miserable.

But, she had to admit, Maida was in the throes of a greater problem. She wished fervently that Maida and Jerry would come to their respective senses instead of going through with a divorce. Maida certainly gave herself away completely every time anything concerning Jerry came up. Karen was convinced that she still loved him.

As for Jerry—she could not believe that he was really willing to blot lovely, excitable, appealingly unpredictable Maida out of his life forever.

She sighed. "If Hugh doesn't mind too much," she said. "I'll stay till you get back from Boston. But after that—"

"We'll face 'after that' when we get to it," Maida said, almost smugly.

It was not until she saw Maida's car round the bend the next morning that Karen began to berate herself for having succumbed to her cousin's wishes so easily.

She poured herself a second cup of coffee and took it into the living room, standing at the window to watch the lake reflect the beginning of a new day.

As she watched, a figure crossed her path of vision. Michael Stanhope was walking along the lakefront path, his hands in the pockets of the heavy, dark green jacket he was wearing, his head down. Karen stared at him, and felt a stab of near-physical pain. There was an air of loneliness and desolation about him, a dejection that touched a deep chord within her.

She was wearing her fleecy pink robe with matching

scuffs, and without even stopping to think, she ran out the door and across the steps that led to the lakefront, and called out his name.

He stopped to look up at her, and still yielding to impulse, she started down the steps toward him, his warning shout reaching her just a second too late. Then everything happened so fast that Karen felt herself falling before she could even begin to make the effort to grab at something to break her plunge.

The world seemed to spin around, and it was a long moment before she realized he had caught her in his arms. He was holding her close to him, murmuring broken little phrases she couldn't quite fathom over and over again as he stroked her hair. She was sure that he had called her "dearest"; she thought he'd said "Oh, my darling"; certainly there was no doubt about the unadulterated emotion in his voice. Karen began to relax, a deliciously warm feeling, increasingly sensuous as it intensified, coming to take possession of her.

Then he put her down so hastily that she rocked on her feet and he said angrily, "Jerry should have had those damned things fixed a long time ago!"

He frowned, slowly started up the steps himself, then stopped and swore.

"The second one from the top's so rotten it's given way entirely," he told her. He held out a hand. "Climb up after me, and step over it."

She obeyed him as if she were a child placed in his care. Once safe at the top, she paused to look back down to the pebbly stretch of sand below them and she really noticed, for the first time, the large boulders to one side of the steps at the bottom. Had she fallen the entire length she could easily have hit square upon them. The mere thought was unnerving!

Michael, following her gaze, said under his breath, "You could have been hurt very badly this time. Dammit, you do seem to be accident prone!"

"That's not so!" she retorted defensively.

The tenderness that had been so much a part of him a moment before was gone, and he stared down at her almost coldly. "I don't agree," he said bluntly. "Can you walk?"

Karen took a tentative step. "Yes. You broke my fall." She hesitated. "You could have been hurt yourself."

He shrugged. "Is Maida still asleep?" he asked her.

"No. Maida's gone to Boston for a couple of days."

There was a chill to the early morning air. She shivered, and Michael said abruptly, "Let's get you back to the house."

He followed her into the living room to ask abruptly, "Does Maida have any brandy?"

"I think so," she told him, "but it's rather early in the day for brandy, isn't it?"

"Not under the circumstances." His lips twisted in a heart-tugging smile. "I'm beginning to feel I should carry a keg of it around my neck while you're around, the way the Saint Bernards who were once used for rescue work in the Alps did."

"That really isn't very funny," she said coldly.

"I wasn't trying to be funny. God, you're trembling!"

She was indeed trembling but it was by no means due entirely to the chill in the air or to her recent experience, and she was glad that he was evidently unaware of this. She followed his instructions, settling into the armchair while he found a blanket and wrapped it around her legs, but she knew only too well that this wasn't what was needed to make her warm.

Michael went out into the kitchen and brought back a bottle half full of brandy, and two glasses.

"Here," he said, thrusting a glass out at her, and this time she took it with her left hand; she didn't dare trust her right.

He pulled up a hassock and sat down on it, looking up at her, and Karen saw that his face was etched with lines of fatigue. She doubted if he'd had much sleep and she wondered if he too suffered from recurring nightmares, as she had until recently.

"Why didn't you leave when Maida did?" he asked her.

"Is my being here that annoying to you?" she countered at his question's sting.

"I didn't say that," he pointed out levelly. "And, in any event, my opinion doesn't matter."

"Doesn't it?"

"There's no reason why it should."

"Do you *always* underrate yourself?"

"I don't attempt to do anything to myself," he told her wearily. "I merely try to get from one day to the next. Sometimes that's more than enough."

"So you go on shunning people, despising people, because you've been in prison and you've built up a hate complex, is that it?" she flung at him, all her mixed feelings about him surfacing so that she was too wrought emotionally to be cautious about what she said to him.

The silence became acute. Then he said, "No. I'll admit I have a tendency to try to avoid people, but I don't think I despise anyone, and I wouldn't say I've built up a hate complex. I just want to be left alone. Is that so hard to understand?"

"It's understandable, perhaps, but it isn't...right," she said stubbornly.

He didn't answer. After a moment he refilled their brandy glasses almost absently, then sat staring into his, twirling the stem and watching the clear brown liquid make a little whirlpool.

He said, without looking at her, "I think I'm beginning to know what your problem is. You're an incurable romantic, Karen."

She was thoroughly surprised. "I?" she demanded.

"Yes, you. I've nothing against romantics, but I think you should know I'm not good material for you." He continued to avoid her eyes, still staring at the brandy. "My crime," he said deliberately, "isn't something that can be exorcised."

She held her breath, because it was so crucial to say the right thing to him. She ventured timidly, "I can appreciate that. But...you have paid for it."

"By serving a term in prison?" he asked caustically. "Do you *really* think I should be able to pick up the pieces and go on from here?" He shook his head. "It's not that simple," he told her, and there was a terrible bleakness in his green eyes. "I *killed* Chad."

"Michael—"

"Let me talk about it." He added under his breath, "I never have before."

"All right, then," she said, catching her own breath. "But I still say you've paid the price that was asked of you. Furthermore, you don't even remember what happened, do you?"

"No," he agreed, "I don't. But I remember the aftermath, the horror, the trial. I remember my mother coming to see me the first day in prison. She never made it home. She suffered the coronary that killed her not fifteen minutes after she left me. Even my father—he was tired, shaken, grief stricken, or he might never have crashed his car. He might be walking around today instead of being confined to a wheelchair for the rest of his life."

"So," Karen said, and wondered where she found the strength to say it, "Because of all this you whip yourself daily, don't you? It's a kind of mental flagellation."

"No," he said, and now he did look directly at her, and there was strength in every line of his face, in the set of his shoulders. True character, as well as that tremendous aura of purely masculine virility and vitality that she found so overpowering.

"I don't wallow in guilt and misery, Karen," he said slowly. "I came here last fall when I was paroled because I felt Dad both wanted and needed me. Now I wonder, sometimes, if it might not have been better for him if I had stayed away. I'm a handicap in many ways. Regardless, though, I'll stick it out through the summer. I have a lot of thinking to do, and this is a good place to do it in. By fall, I hope to come to some sort of decision, I hope to find a course to follow. But it's going to be a long road, a very long road, and one I am going to have to travel on my own."

He smiled faintly, and she ached for him. He said,

"I wanted to tell you at least some of this out on the island yesterday, but it was difficult. You see, for three years I spoke very little. I ate, I slept, I worked in the prison hospital, and I was glad they gave me a chance to do something useful. I didn't have time to sit around staring at blank walls, but I did get into a habit of silence and it isn't an easy habit to break. When I do break it, more often than not I say all the wrong things." His smile became wry. "I think you know that."

"Michael," she began, this on a decided note of protest, and he shook his head.

"No, let me finish. You—you must stop trying to find excuses for me, Karen. I appreciate your efforts, but since I've met you I've come to realize even more than I did before that for the rest of my life I'm going to have to face up to the fact that I'm an ex-convict. That can never be changed."

A bleakness had come over his face, an expression she'd seen there all too often in the short time she'd known him. She said, faltering over the words, "I've dredged all of this up for you. That wasn't my intention, Michael. It wasn't my intention at all. I—I'm very sorry."

He shrugged slightly. "You may be sorry, but you should realize, Karen, that you can't expect to probe into anyone's past without doing some dredging at the same time. That's the trouble with romantics like yourself. You tend to glamorize everything, you try to look at life through the proverbial rose-colored glasses...and it isn't like that. I should think you'd long since have recognized that fact from your own experiences. But you're still a believer, aren't you?

You still believe in happy-ever-after endings, and the beautiful princess and the handsome prince."

She remembered her musings about Sleeping Beauty and Prince Charming and felt her cheeks growing hot. Was Michael Stanhope a mind reader, among other things?

Karen knew that her face tended to be much too revealing. Friends had often told her that she was very poor at camouflaging her emotions, but until now it never had mattered to her. Now, though, she wished that she could find it possible to conceal both thoughts and feelings from Michael, and she was glad that he seemed so self-absorbed at the moment that he wasn't looking at her.

"Let me tell you, Karen, there is nothing glamorous about prison, nor is it an experience anyone can hope to forget from the first moment you see those walls and know that you are going to be behind them."

She shrank from the bitterness of his tone as he continued. "Those walls, believe me, are the end of the world. They're higher than life, and when you go through the gate and hear it shut behind you it's like no other sound. After that, what I'll call the real indignities begin. I'm not about to go into them. . . . I don't want to speak of them to you, to anyone."

He stood and moved restlessly to the window, and it seemed to her that in a few short steps he had put an abyss between them too vast for any bridge. He turned to glance down at her with an expression that was frightening in its iciness.

"What could you possibly know about that kind of a private hell? How could you possibly understand what it means to lose your freedom? I even had to get my parole officer's permission to leave Massachusetts and come up here to Vermont. I had to get permission to drive a car, to *breathe*. Are you telling me that someone like you can even begin to know what that's like?"

"No," she said, her voice so tight she could barely speak. "I can only imagine—"

"Imagine!" he scoffed harshly. "There isn't that much imagination in the world!"

He put down the brandy glass and stood before her, towering over her, tall, straight, and as taut as a poised arrow. "Yesterday was a mistake. You're a very attractive woman. You must know that. Certainly you've made other men lose control, you came close to making me lose control too, but it won't happen again. There's no place in my life for you, and certainly none in yours for me. For God's sake, *remember* that, will you?"

Chapter Nine

Maida had promised that she would telephone before the day was over to tell Karen exactly how long she needed to stay in Boston.

But Maida, Karen knew, was apt to be forgetful about such things, especially when she was preoccupied with her own affairs. And now she determined that if she hadn't heard from her cousin by evening she would start making phone calls of her own, even if it meant contacting Jerry and asking him to find Maida for her.

After this latest encounter with Michael, it was impossible to contemplate staying on Grand Isle much longer.

He'd stalked out of the house after that final, explosive statement in which he'd told her—leaving no doubt about it—that there was no place in his life for her. She had sat very still for a long time once he'd gone, this no indication at all of the turmoil that was raging within her.

Somehow, Michael managed to tear her apart emotionally in one way or another every time they met.

And, she thought wryly, until she met him she'd really had no idea how many different emotional ways there were in which one could be profoundly affected!

She knew that if she'd been the slightest bit encouraging she would not have been able to escape continuing on a path that common sense told her was pitted with rocks for her to stumble over. But he'd not been the slightest bit encouraging! Very much the opposite.

She wished, dully, that she'd been able to leave the first thing this morning, as she'd intended doing. Then this last, bruising session with Michael would have been avoided. It would have been much easier to have left on a note of being slightly jealous of his relationship with June Kensington. But now....

"Blast Maida!" Karen said this aloud, without even realizing it, then heard her own voice speaking into the stillness and was a bit shocked by its sound.

Maida was adorable, there was no doubt of that. It had always been difficult to refuse her anything. That, probably, was part of Jerry's problem too! But there were moments when Maida was blind, in a rather peculiar way. Or so overly concerned with her own affairs that she simply didn't see what was happening to the other people around her.

Maida should have known that she wanted to get out of there and must have had a really good reason for feeling that way, Karen thought, a bit resentfully. It would have been smarter, she conceded to herself, if she'd pretended to be having an ongoing romance with Hugh MacKnight. Maida would have been able to understand her eagerness to get back to New York then. As it was, it was going to be hard to think of a valid excuse if Maida called and said that she was in a tangle of her own in Boston that had to be straightened out.

"Well," Karen said, again speaking into the stillness, "I shall simply tell her I have to get back to my job, that's all. And that I'll leave the key to the house with Judge Stanhope and ask Horace to keep an eye on the place."

Thinking of the judge made her remember his invitation to come and look at the mineral collection, and this was something she really wanted to do. She hesitated to go over to the big, spruce-colored house on the bluff, true, knowing that Michael might be there. Yet, she decided defiantly, there was no reason why she should forgo the pleasure of seeing the judge one more time, and his late wife's collection as well, in order to avoid Michael. He could stay out of her way if he didn't want to face her again!

The judge had not specified a particular time of day in which she should call on him, and after thinking it over, Karen decided that there was nothing wrong with the present. The middle of the morning would probably suit the judge as well as any time.

She nearly phoned him first to be sure of this because she didn't want to inconvenience him. But then she decided against it because there was the chance that Michael might answer the phone and even invent some excuse to keep her from coming so that there wouldn't be a need for another confrontation.

Because she had no wish to encounter either Rod or June Kensington at the moment either, Karen walked down to the fork in the road instead of taking the short cut through the woods, and then continued along the other branch to the crescent driveway in front of the big house.

She hesitated a moment before lifting the bronze knocker. Her memory of her first reception on these premises was still much too vivid! But this time once she'd let the knocker fall it was Horace who answered, looking as ugly and impassive as ever.

He took her through the living room, and she looked longingly at the piano, wishing that she had the courage to accept the judge's invitation to play it. This time they followed the corridor at the end opposite the hall that led to the judge's library, passing a dining room to the right, overlooking the lake, then a large, spotless kitchen, and coming finally to the circular end room that was the counterpart of the room in which she and Maida had had cocktails.

This, though, was a workshop. The walls were lined with multidrawered wooden cabinets, while a long pine table was centered in the floor. The table was piled with books and papers, and the judge sat at one end of it.

His welcome was so warm that it dispelled all her doubts about coming. He glanced at his watch and said, "Just in time for my coffee break! Shall we have it in here or in the living room?"

Karen did not want to be close to the piano again so she said, "Here, if you don't mind," and added, this with sincerity, "I'm fascinated by all this."

The judge laughed. "Wait till I show you my treasures!"

Horace brought coffee and cinnamon buns, and the judge cleared away space on the table for them, inviting Karen to draw up a chair.

The cinnamon buns were freshly baked and delicious and Karen was surprised when the judge told her with a twinkle that it was Horace who had made them. Horace also made a superb cup of coffee, and as she chatted casually with the judge, Karen readily accepted a second cup, and a second bun as well.

The break finished, the judge took her on an inspection tour of his premises, rolling his wheelchair from one cabinet to another as he opened drawer after drawer, each one revealing new delights.

Karen drew in her breath with pleasure and astonishment so many times that the judge finally said, "Karen, you amaze me! You really do love these things, don't you? You react to them the same way my Eleanor used to."

"I guess I can thank my father, at least in part, for having introduced me to the world of minerals and gems at an early age," she admitted, "but they *are* so beautiful."

She picked up a chunk of sulfur crystals, glistening and purest yellow in color. She exclaimed over a specimen of azurite, blue at the edges and ranging to deepest purple, and the judge told her that he and his wife had found it on a holiday in Arizona. There were exquisite garnets, which they had discovered in Connecticut and, to her surprise, sapphires that Mrs. Stanhope had found in Montana.

"I know," the judge nodded. "You usually think of sapphires coming from more exotic places, like Ceylon and Burma."

In all, there were thousands of specimens, eclipsing the rainbow in their range of color. The variety of shapes and sizes also seemed near-infinite, and some of the minerals were opalescent, some opaque, some with the prism clarity of crystal quartz. And there was gold, nuggets of rich, gleaming gold, that had come from Colorado and California and Australia.

When the judge learned that Karen's birthday was in August, he insisted upon giving her a peridot. It had been cut and faceted, and glowed with pure green fire. Karen was reminded of the stone she had seen in the jeweler's window in New York and coveted, but this peridot reminded her even more of Michael's eyes. She felt that she had never in her life wanted anything more, and yet she insisted that she couldn't accept it.

When she declined, the judge momentarily looked as sad as she imagined he must often feel despite the cheerful front he put up. "Please, my dear. Eleanor would want you to have it. You and she would have delighted in each other's company. I'll have it set in a ring or pendant for you, whichever you wish."

She hesitated only briefly, and then capitulated. "I should truly love to have the stone," she confessed, "but I do insist on having it mounted myself. And I shall wear it always, once I do."

He was touched. So, for that matter, was she. He took her hand in a silent moment of deep affinity, and her heart went out to this proud, wonderful man.

She was thoroughly startled when someone said, "Dad!" She and the judge both looked up to see Michael standing in the doorway.

Karen could feel her throat tighten, an affliction she seemed to encounter every time she saw him. Their eyes meshed, and she knew that this was not entirely a one-sided impact. Michael Stanhope, no matter what he might say about having no place in his life for her, was certainly as thoroughly aware of her as she was of him.

Nevertheless, there was no welcome in those peridot eyes and he said stiffly, "I'm sorry. I didn't know you were here, Karen. I didn't mean to interrupt."

"You're not interrupting," the judge put in swiftly. "I've been showing Karen your mother's collection— and I might say that I've never had a more appreciative audience."

Michael walked across the room slowly, his face inscrutable. He glanced at the open drawer from which the judge had taken the peridot and said, "They *are* beautiful, aren't they? When I was a kid, mother used to let me play with them on rainy days, rare though some of them are." He glanced at the stone she was holding. "You like peridots?" he asked her.

"Yes," she said. "They're my birthstone, and I love them. Your father is insisting upon giving me this beautiful one. Tell him I shouldn't let him do it, will you?"

Michael smiled, a very slight smile, but she found herself clinging to it. "No," he said, "I will not tell him anything of the kind. I'd say that Dad has very good taste, and that he has chosen the perfect recipient for it."

Before Karen could recover from this, Michael turned to his father. "Dad, I noticed you had some of those colored marking pencils in here the other day. Could I borrow a couple? I promised Ambrose I'd make him a map."

To her further surprise, he turned to Karen to explain, as casually as if this morning's encounter between them had never happened. "There's an English warship at the bottom of the lake that dates back to the War of 1812. I've done some diving around it in the past, and now Ambrose says he wants to do the same thing when he's old enough, though thank God he's promised to wait till I make the decision about that! Nevertheless, he insists I do an 'X marks the spot' rendition for him."

The judge rummaged among the papers on his desk and found a selection of colored pencils. "Will these do?" he asked.

"They're perfect," Michael said. As he took them, he added, "Will you both excuse me?" Then, without waiting for an answer, he left them.

Karen, looking after him, soon realized that she must be revealing more in her expression than she wanted to do, for the judge said quietly, "You like him, don't you?"

She faced a pair of wise blue eyes looking up at her. And, swallowing hard, she admitted, "Yes, I do."

"You're having quite an effect on him," the judge said slowly. "He's had a rough going, Karen. During the course of it, he's built a wall around himself. The wall is still there, to be sure, but I would say that there definitely is a crack in it. If for nothing else, I will be eternally grateful to you for that, my dear."

Before she could respond, he quickly changed the subject, turning his wheelchair around and propelling it to another section of the cabinet-lined wall.

"Now," he said, "you must see some other treasures. These, plus the gold, make up the real value of this collection, though Eleanor was equally fond of the less costly items. I doubt she would have traded a piece of onyx she once found in a cave in New Mexico for any of these.''

The judge pulled open a drawer to reveal emeralds and rubies, star sapphires, moonstones, aquamarines.

"None of these stones, of course, are as famous as the Hope Diamond or the Star of the East,'' the judge said. "A few do have interesting histories of their own, though, which I intend to write up and present with them. Actually, they belong to Michael; they were a part of his inheritance from his mother. But he has told me he wishes them to go to the museum with the other things. He feels that the entire collection belongs together.''

"But they must be worth a fortune!'' Karen exclaimed, dazzled.

"Yes, today they are,'' the judge agreed. "Of course we acquired them over a period of years, a stone at a time, as we did the gold. The value has skyrocketed, I realize that. This is one reason why I am anxious to complete my work, in one sense. In another sense, in the sense of the pleasure it gives me, I wish it might go on forever. While I am working with the things she loved, I feel especially close to Eleanor.''

He shrugged. "That's as it may be,'' he said firmly. "The practical fact of the matter is that the insurance I have on the collection no longer covers more than a fraction of its true worth. Even in a location as remote as this, there is always danger of theft, to say nothing of fire. These treasures should be in a safer place. Also, they should be inventoried and the scattered notes Eleanor made about them correlated. It presents quite a task.''

Karen hesitated, then she said, "Judge Stanhope, wouldn't this go faster if you had someone to type for you?"

"Indeed it would," he agreed. "But, as I mentioned to you the other day, that is a skill neither Horace nor I have ever acquired, nor has Michael, and I think you can understand that I don't relish bringing a stranger into this."

"I type," Karen found herself saying. And when he looked at her questioningly, she added, "My surgeon advocated a typing course after the last operation on my arm, and I've been working in his office since, typing, among other things, as a kind of therapy. I don't know just how long I'm going to stay here on Grand Isle, in fact I expected originally that I'd be back in New York by now."

She paused, astonished at herself for going this far. All her resolves about leaving the farmhouse untended seemed to be vanishing into thin air! She plunged on. "I've a feeling that Maida isn't going to let me go easily," and that was true enough. "She seems almost desperate for company. So, as long as I *am* here, I'd be delighted to type up your notes for you."

She held her breath after this speech, afraid to look at him. Then she heard him laugh and saw that his blue eyes were twinkling.

"I'd been hoping you would suggest exactly that!" he confessed.

Karen and the judge agreed that there was no point in postponing their starting to work together. Horace was sent to the attic to unearth a typewriter that had performed yeoman service for a number of years in the judge's law office. It was of a considerably older vintage than the machine Karen had become accustomed to in Hugh MacKnight's office, but she quickly grew used to it.

Lunchtime came, and again papers were cleared from the big pine table and Horace brought them delicious chicken salad sandwiches, a tangy tomato bisque, and hot gingerbread topped with freshly whipped cream.

To Karen's disappointment, Michael didn't join them. She was tempted to ask the judge whether he usually lunched alone, or whether his absence was due to her presence. Caution triumphed, though, and she decided against revealing that much curiosity.

The afternoon passed quickly. At four o'clock the judge suggested either a cup of tea or perhaps one of Horace's special daiquiries. But Karen, having decided that there was such a thing as using up too much of someone's hospitality even if you *were* doing volunteer work for them, refused with a definite sense of regret and insisted that she had to get back to Maida's house.

It was as well, because shortly after she arrived, Maida phoned. She sounded depressed. The session with the lawyer had been more traumatic than she had expected it to be and she admitted that her spirits were very low. She also said that she planned to start back for Grand Isle the first thing in the morning. "But please," she begged, "don't leave just because I'm coming back, Karen. Not right away, at least."

Karen deliberated telling her cousin about her work with Judge Stanhope, then decided it would be better to go into it once Maida was in residence again. She suspected that although Maida was fond of the judge she might not be particularly enthusiastic about Karen's working in the house in which Michael Stanhope was living.

She compromised by saying, "Don't worry, darling, I won't rush off, I promise you. We'll talk about it when you get here."

She hung up, made herself a cup of tea and picked up the mystery novel she had been reading, but shortly thereafter set it aside again. She was restless and more than a little despondent herself. Maida's troubles had caused a sorry sort of echo.

The evening stretched before her, and for the first time she wished that there were a television set in the house. Toward sunset she thought of taking a walk along the lakefront, yet she knew that to do so would only make her yearn all the more for the companionship she didn't have. She would be hoping to suddenly come upon Michael, while at the same time dreading that she might do so.

She heated a can of soup for supper, then went back to the book again. It was nearly eight when someone knocked vigorously at the kitchen door, and she opened it to find Rod Kensington standing at the threshold.

"Don't look so startled!" He grinned. "I'm not the bogeyman."

"Sorry," she apologized. "I guess I'm just not used to being alone in the country."

"Has Maida gone somewhere?"

"Yes, to Boston. She'll be back tomorrow, though."

"I noticed her car wasn't here," Rod said. "You

should have told us you'd be alone. June and I would have liked to have had you come over for dinner. Matter of fact, why don't you come back and have a drink with us?"

"Thanks," Karen said, then added, because the thought really didn't appeal, "I'd appreciate a raincheck, though. I think I'll take a shower and turn in."

Rod smiled. "Was your day with the judge all that taxing?" he asked her.

She stared at him. "What?"

He chuckled at her astonishment. "Karen, you can't hope to keep your comings and goings secret! There's a gap in the trees between the judge's place and ours. June was looking out the window this morning and saw you go next door, and hours later she happened to glance out to see you coming out of the house. Matter of fact," he confessed, "she's burning up with curiosity."

"Oh?"

Rod surveyed her closely. "You seem annoyed," he said.

"I am a bit annoyed, Rod. I don't like to be spied upon."

"That's a strong word," he protested ruefully. "It wasn't intentional. I think primarily June is wondering if Michael was there too—I presume it *was* the judge you were with?"

"Yes," Karen said coldly, "it was the judge. And, yes, Michael was there too. You might as well tell June that I plan to be with the judge on a daily basis as long as I stay on Grand Isle. I'm working with him, as a matter of fact."

"Doing what, if I'm not being too nosy?"

"Cataloging his wife's mineral collection. He plans to present it to a museum in New York."

Rod whistled softly. "You really got into the old man's confidence quickly," he observed, to her further annoyance. "He's usually pretty private about anything involving Aunt Eleanor. What does Michael think about all this?"

"I don't know," Karen said bluntly. "We didn't consult him. If your sister is curious about his opinion, why doesn't she ask him?"

"Come on!" Rod cajoled her. "I've really rubbed you the wrong way—which is precisely what I didn't want to do. How about me taking you to some nice country inn for breakfast tomorrow morning?"

"Sorry," she said, "but I have a job to do!"

Rod did his best to be charming for the next few minutes, and she realized he was hoping that she would relent to the point of asking him in for coffee, or a drink, but he really had annoyed her. Or to be more precise about it, she admitted to herself once he had left, June Kensington's proprietory interest where Michael was concerned put her off completely!

Maida, she realized, must know the true story of whatever involvement there had been between Michael and June in the past. Karen made up her mind to question her cousin about this as soon as an opportunity arose in which she could do so without being obvious.

Shortly after nine o'clock the next morning Karen walked up to the fork in the road, and then down the other branch to the judge's house. Before she could knock, the door opened and Horace said, "Good morning, ma'am. The judge was just trying to phone you."

"Karen," the judge called, propelling himself across the foyer in his wheelchair. "I forgot to tell you yesterday that I have a dental appointment in Burlington this morning. Go right ahead, anyway, won't you? The house is all yours. Just don't begin to think I'm too much of a slave driver, that's all! I've left a stack of material for you that will take a week of hard labor to complete!"

Karen laughed and promised him that she would proceed at her own pace.

As she walked down the corridor to the circular workroom, she wondered if Michael were around or if he had possibly taken Ambrose off on another expedition of some sort.

The judge had, indeed, left a stack of material for her. As she worked on it, she began to evolve a system. And there was definite satisfaction in bringing together what had been a scrambled mass of data into the beginning of an integrated whole. This collection deserved proper presentation, with enough information about each specimen so that both scientist and layman could appreciate it to the fullest.

It was concentrated work. By eleven o'clock, when she had been at it for the better part of two hours, Karen found herself beginning to get restless, despite her interest in what she was doing. And this restlessness, she knew, was augmented by hunger pangs, since she had not bothered with breakfast this morning.

Horace had told her that there was coffee and homemade crullers in the kitchen and had urged her to help herself. Now she did so and was impressed by Horace's housekeeping ability. The kitchen was immaculate, and the crullers were delicious.

As she sat at the white-painted wooden table, Karen wondered about Horace and how he came to be here. He looked like such a brute of a man. Despite the fact that he was unfailingly polite to her she still felt somewhat uncomfortable around him. Perhaps, she conceded, this was because she sensed that he felt uncomfortable around *her*.

Karen finished the coffee and rinsed out her cup. Then, instead of going directly back to the workroom, she found herself wandering down the corridor and on into the living room.

She paused by the piano, her longing for the beautiful instrument she had always loved—and had made her career choice—surfacing. Impulsively she reached down, using her left hand, and rippled an arpeggio. Then, very tentatively, she lowered her right hand toward the keyboard and played a scale, just the scale of C, the simplest scale of all, and slowly at that. But when she had finished, she drew a deep breath. It had worked! Her fingers had responded. Hugh Mac-Knight, bless him, had been right! All this time she had been building her finger dexterity. Essentially the same movements were involved in typing and playing a piano; at least they were sufficiently related so that proficiency in one could definitely have an effect upon proficiency in the other.

She pulled out the bench, sat down, and, holding her breath, began to play, warning herself to do something fairly easy. She chose Brahms's "Lullaby," playing it slowly, softly. Naturally there was not the finesse there had been, not the freedom. She decided analytically that the problem lay mainly with her wrist, which would have to be worked upon. Exercises, she thought. She must ask Hugh about a program of exercises that would build up strength in the wrist while further conditioning both her fingers and her arms.

Then she sat back, enraptured. It was incredible, but she was *playing!*

Now she drifted into a Chopin nocturne—not half bad, considering, she told herself—and then relaxed with Rota's theme from *Romeo and Juliet*. As she played the last chord, she was suddenly aware that she was being watched. She turned, knowing who it was even before she saw Michael leaning against the wall.

Briefly she was so stunned by the pure impact of his physical presence that she could think of nothing else. He was wearing snug-fitting jeans and a light gray knit shirt that molded his arms and shoulders while emphasizing the color of his hair. But it was a most attractive emphasis.

She became aware that she was staring at him, and she said reprovingly, shaking her head slightly, "How long have you been there?"

"From the middle of Brahms through Chopin and on into Rota," he told her.

"You should have said something!"

"I wasn't about to interrupt." He surveyed her steadily, then said softly, "It's still there, isn't it? Right in your fingertips. Somehow I was sure it would be."

"I don't know," she told him doubtfully. "I'm not all that sure myself. There's a way to go. A long way to go."

"But you'll be back at it," he insisted. "I guarantee that you'll be back on the concert stage where you belong within the next year."

Where she belonged? *Was* that where she still belonged? she wondered. She looked down at her hands and wriggled her fingers. She'd had several years of playing concerts, touring from coast to coast, going on throughout Europe and the British Isles, living from hotel to hotel. Before that, it seemed to her as if she had been having an affair with the piano ever since she could remember. She had sat at the bench hour after hour as a child. She had wanted it that way, to be sure; she had loved this instrument, which, under her fingers, seemed to possess a life entirely of its own. But she was also aware that there had been experiences missed. Playing with other children, for one thing. And birthday parties when, for instance, she was getting ready for a recital. She'd never been encouraged to participate in sports, because there was always the chance that she might injure her hands, and even a broken finger could have been disastrous.

As a teen-ager she had followed an early-to-bed regime, because rising young concert artists needed their rest. She knew that sometimes her father had been appalled by her schedule. It was he who had taken her fishing with him and had taught her how to catch a ball—admittedly behind her mother's back—and had showed her that there was more to life than sharps and flats and beautiful music.

Did she *want* to go back on the concert stage again?

She said slowly, "I don't know. I'm not sure it *is* where I belong."

"You've lost confidence," Michael said, "but that

will come back too, and then you'll *know* it's where you belong, without any doubt." His lips twisted in a rueful smile. "It will be just a matter of time."

"Suppose," Karen said slowly, "that I decide I don't want to go back on the concert stage, even if I'm able to."

"I'd find that unbelievable."

"Would you?"

Their eyes fused, and his darkened as he looked at her. "Karen," he began, "you shouldn't—"

But he was not to finish his thought—whatever it was. Without even realizing it, she stood, and the space between them seemed to close of its own accord. Her arms went out to him and he drew her to him, holding her so tightly that she felt as if their pulses were merging into a single, deep beat.

His lips found hers, but this time tenderness merged with passion, and they moved with a single intent toward the same couch upon which he had placed her after the accident. He lowered her as gently now as he had then but this time he came to join her, pressing her against him so that their bodies seemed to mold, to fuse, and she responded to him with an instinctive arching, wanting him as she had never wanted anyone before.

His hands explored her, those wonderful fingers setting forth on a quest so evocative that she felt herself filled with a soaring rapture that was sweeter than music. Gradually she found herself impelled to touch him even as he was touching her, and, with slow deliberation, she unbuttoned his shirt, pressing her lips to his chest. Then her fingers began to seek further while simultaneously he unzipped her slacks, caressing her with an invasive intimacy that carried with it its own brand of fire.

She felt as if she were being carried along on a molten flow of such warmth and beauty that she was not sure she could bear the intensity of it, even as she reveled in its glory. And the shock was brutal when suddenly he thrust her away from him. He lay at her side for a moment, his breath coming in retching gasps, but she was too bewildered to appreciate his agony. It was impossible, at this instant, to go beyond, that far beyond herself, in the wake of abandoned passion.

Finally she whispered, "What is it?"

Michael turned on her violently. "What is it? What the hell do you *think* it is?" he demanded. "We must both be insane!"

He got to his feet and strode across to the window. For an endless moment he stood with his back to her. Then he shuddered once, a convulsive shudder that was an echo of her own seething turmoil.

"I thought I'd spelled it out for you," he said thickly. "But you didn't get the message, did you? You can't *believe* I don't want you in my life! Okay, I'm to blame too this time. But it won't happen again, that I promise you. It will never happen again!"

Chapter Ten

Again Michael left her in anger, and as she slowly began to rally, Karen told herself, this not without bitterness, that it was getting to be a habit.

Why? That was the question that plagued her the most. He seemed as impelled toward her as she was toward him. Whatever else she could deny she surely could not deny the tremendous tug of the physical attraction they had for each other. Despite his assurances that he didn't want her in his life he seemed as unable to keep from taking her in his arms as she was to fall into them when opportunity presented itself.

Yet, so far, he had managed to exercise a self-control she found difficult to understand. Was that what being in prison did to a person? Did men—or did a particular man—become part human, part robot?

Michael seemed able to switch from passion to something close to iciness very swiftly. She couldn't say that it was something he did with ease because, remembering, she knew now that he had been deeply tormented after putting pause to a situation that, Karen had to admit, would have led to only one conclusion.

Yet he had wanted that conclusion, she was sure of it. And she had wanted it too. She had wanted to know the fullness of a total experience between them, a culmination as old as man and woman.

She still found this hard to believe, but it was true. She had wanted Michael; she had wanted him with a surpassing urgency. She shivered as she thought of it, and shivered even more when the realization of something else swept over her.

This was not an entirely sensual reaction. This was not merely the desire for satisfaction of an appetite purely sexual. It went beyond that, she knew that now, and it was terrifying knowledge. Because it meant that this was not a case of physical attraction—even powerful physical attraction—and nothing more.

I love him, Karen thought, and tears came to sting her eyes as she repeated this to herself again. *I love him! And he doesn't want me. I don't think he wants any woman as part of his life. He feels he has to go it alone, all the rest of the way. Whatever course he's going to follow must be a solitary one, he's told me that. But still....*

She shook her head, staring bleakly across at the piano that had, in a way, started this whole episode today. If Michael had not heard her playing he would not have sought her out, she was reasonably sure of that. Her music had attracted him; he'd already let her know that he was a music lover. He still remembered a concert she'd given once in Boston.

So today it was Brahms who had lured him first. And it had gone on from there.

But where was it going to lead to? Despite his actions, despite his insistence, Karen could not let her-

self believe that he was really going to make this the
end of the road for both of them.

If so, she thought dully, *I can't believe that there's
ever going to be another route I'll really want to follow!*

It was with an effort that she went back to work in
the judge's office. Even though she was fascinated
with the subject matter, she found it almost impossible to concentrate, and was relieved when the judge
came back shortly after one o'clock.

The dental session had unfortunately left him with
a sore jaw. Although he tried to do justice to the late
lunch Horace had prepared, he concluded ruefully
that a man his age might actually be bettbr off with
false teeth.

Karen had no aching jaw to blame her lack of appetite on and tried to use the coffee-and-crullers snack
as an excuse. But she had the feeling that she wasn't
fooling Horace.

Toward midafternoon, his jaw still paining him, the
judge decided to take a nap. Karen seized this opportunity to suggest that she too call it a day. She told the
judge that she felt she'd exercised her arm enough for
one day, and he quickly agreed that it was wise not to
push it.

She'd gotten back some measure of emotional control, yet as she walked around the long way back to
the farmhouse she felt as if her nerves were ragged. It
was too familiar a feeling, and she began to think that
Hugh MacKnight hadn't been very wise at all when
he'd prescribed "involvement" for her.

She'd been in the house only a few minutes when
the phone rang and it was Maida, still in Boston.

"I overslept this morning, so I decided to stay and do

some shopping," Maida confessed. Then she added hastily, "But I'll get an early start back tomorrow."

Karen was too tired to protest about this, even though she felt she should, if only as a kind of self-defense. But then she realized that her resentment was not stemming nearly so much from Maida's staying in Boston as from the fact that she had fully intended to get Maida into a conversation tonight that would fill her in on the relationship, both past and present, between Michael and June Kensington.

She soon discovered that this was no time to be alone. She tried to take a nap but could not go to sleep, nor could she concentrate upon the neglected mystery novel. It was impossible to shut Michael out of her thoughts.

Even while he had been telling her today that he would never again make love to her, even while he was assuring her that he didn't want her in his life, she had sensed an anguish in him, a hopelessness, that tore at her.

Now she wished there were someone who could tell her more about the party that night at Chad's and exactly what had happened. Rod and June were possibilities, but she had no desire to broach the subject with either of them. Maida, unfortunately from Karen's present point of view, had not been at Chad's herself. In fact, everything she knew about that terrible night had come to her secondhand. And, unfortunately, there was no one she could turn to for information.

Or was there?

The young doctor in the emergency room at the hospital in Burlington had been at Chad's that night. True, he had left before the shooting. But he still could give her a firsthand account of the party itself and the people who had been there. He might even know the girl who had been with Michael at the time and had been the only witness to testify at the trial.

Karen glanced at her watch. It was not quite six o'clock. Bradley Simmons might be on duty at the hospital, or he might be free. There was only one way to find out.

It took a while to get the call through. Dr. Bradley Simmons had to be paged, and at first he didn't seem to be responding. When he finally did get to the phone, he was out of breath. But he remembered her immediately, and told her that he actually had been on his way out the door when he got her phone call.

"I'm off until 3 P.M. tomorrow," he said.

This exceeded Karen's wildest expectations.

She hesitated. He probably had very little free time, and as far as she knew he might be married and have a wife at home waiting for him.

She said tentatively, "There was something I wanted to ask you about."

"Anything wrong?" he demanded hastily.

"Medically, you mean? No. But there's something else I'd like to see you about. I—I'd want you to keep it confidential, though."

There was no doubt that he was puzzled, nor could she blame him. But after a moment he said, "Perhaps we could get together for dinner or a drink?"

"I'd like that very much," Karen said frankly. "The cousin I'm visiting on Grand Isle is away just now, so I'm free tonight. I'd suggest you come for dinner here, but I'm afraid we're pretty much down to canned soup."

This was true enough. But the real reason she didn't want to arrange a rendezvous at the farmhouse was that she didn't want to risk an accidental meeting between Michael and his friend!

Bradley Simmons laughed. "We'll find a place that offers sustenance," he promised her.

"I have a car," she told him. "I can meet you in Burlington if you like."

"I'd enjoy the trek out there," he said. "Suppose I pick you up in about an hour."

Karen was at the kitchen door when Brad Simmons arrived, and quickly walked down the back steps to join him before he could get out of his car. It went against her grain, as far as hospitality was concerned, not to ask him to come in for a drink, but she didn't want to linger. Nor was this only because of Michael. It had also occurred to her that Rod or June Kensington or both of them might decide to pay an impromptu visit.

Although there was no particular reason for secrecy where Dr. Simmons was concerned she didn't want to be in the position of having to make introductions just now.

It was not until they had turned out of the side road and were driving along Route Two that she began to relax and, in relaxing, realized how very tense she had been and how anxious to get away without encountering anyone.

She settled back with a sigh, and Brad Simmons looked across at her, his dark eyes frankly curious.

"Don't you think you'd better tell me what this is all about?" he suggested.

"I intend to," she said ruefully. "But I don't know quite where to begin."

"The beginning's usually as good a place as any," he suggested mischievously.

She tried to force a laugh, but it didn't work very well. Her lovely face was serious as she said, "Well, it involves Michael Stanhope. The other night at the hospital I felt that you are his friend."

"You were right," he said. "I am."

"You were in school together," she said. "You're the only person I know outside of relatives who knew him at the time of the murder. That's why I called you."

"Does Mike know about this?"

"No. Please, for the moment I don't want him to. I don't want anyone to know I called you. I didn't want anyone to see you come for me, that's why I was in such a hurry. Otherwise I would have asked you in."

Karen drew a long breath. "There was a witness to Chad Stanhope's death, wasn't there? A girl named Susan Foster?"

Brad Simmons frowned. Then he said, "Yes," this reluctantly.

"Did you know her?"

"As a matter of fact, I did."

"Then perhaps you can tell me about her. I know she was Michael's girl. At least that's what my cousin said. So what I'm interested in is where she may be now."

"I'm getting the impression that you want to see her."

Karen nodded. "If I can possibly find her, I do."

"What good could it do? Mike was convicted, he

served time, he's on parole. Nothing can change that. Nothing can wipe it out.''

"The stigma," said Karen. "The guilt. *That* could be changed. Depending, of course, upon what really happened and what she really saw.''

"Susan testified under oath as to what she really saw," Brad Simmons said. "Certainly she had no ax to grind—more's the pity, perhaps. So I'm not sure what you're getting at.''

She said stubbornly, "There has to be some hope for Michael.''

"Hope?" he echoed. "That's an odd way to put it." Then he said, "Look. I know a delightful old inn near here where lights are so dim no one will recognize us. And the food is surprisingly good. We'll have a very strong drink, maybe two. Then you can tell me the whole thing right from the beginning.''

"That's your prescription?" She laughed.

He nodded. "It's got Rx written all over it!"

And they followed it. It was about a twenty-minute drive to the inn and Karen was beginning to feel a bit more relaxed when they got there. It was a charming old place overlooking the lake, and as they were led to a table by the window and Karen looked out at Champlain, swathed, now, in twilight's mauve shadows, she inevitably remembered her first afternoon on Grand Isle when she had sat at the window in Maida's house watching Michael row Ambrose out to the island. Later, the sunset-streaked sky had been at his back on the return trip, a lonely silhouette despite the small boy by his side.

Brad ordered Manhattans on the rocks for both of them and refused to let her speak about anything serious until they were halfway through the drink. Then, finally, she began her story. It was an autobiography in a way, at least in the beginning. She told him about her family, her career, about Maida meeting and marrying Jerry, and about herself meeting and marrying Keith Morse. She told him about the plane crash, the long months of both surgery and convalescence and then working for Hugh MacKnight. She told him of Hugh's prescription for involvement, Maida's phone call coming just at this time, and her response to it. Then Michael. The car incident. Rod Kensington, and his sister, June.

She did not detail her feelings about June's involvement, either past, present or both, with Michael.

Karen told Brad Simmons about the judge's near-priceless mineral and gem collection, and her own part in helping him catalog it. Then there was Horace, who was such a mystery man. One couldn't help but be curious about Horace. And there was Ambrose, a terrific youngster who adored Michael and to whom Michael surely related well. But it wasn't enough, she said, pain in her lovely amber eyes, to limit yourself to companionship with one small boy when you were young and vital and had as much to offer the world as Michael had. . . .

At this, Brad Simmons smiled almost wistfully and said, "Lucky Michael."

"Lucky?"

"He's lucky to have you on his side." He finished his drink, then beckoned the waitress to bring a second round. "You know, it seems to me that sometimes people like yourself who have been through their own kind of hell develop an added perception. A seventh sense, shall we say?'' He laughed. "I suppose that seems pretty unscientific, yet I've seen it happen more than once.

"In Michael's case, I can understand why you find it difficult to believe the facts, but they *are* there. I'm not going to lure you into any false hopes for yourself, to say nothing of Michael. It was hard enough for *me* to believe what happened at the time. Mike and I were both doing our residency, though in different fields, but we had been classmates in med school. I was sharing an apartment at the time with two other guys, and I didn't hear about Chad's death until the next day, when I went on duty at the hospital. I'll never forget it.

"I'd had a date the night before, frankly we had our own thing to do and so although we did stop at Chad's party we did so only briefly. Chad was fuming because Michael was supposed to bring an extra supply of liquor. He was late, and they were running dry.

"I remember telling Chad that Mike probably hadn't been able to get away from the hospital. I remember joking about the way he still had it easy as a med student, but he'd find out what life was like by the time he got as far as residency."

Brad shook his head. "Those words have often come back to haunt me," he admitted. "Chad found out what *death* was like, not long after I left him."

The waitress put the fresh drinks before them and Karen said, "If this girl Susan really did tell the truth on the witness stand, doesn't it seem that Michael must have had some *reason* for pulling the trigger on that gun?"

"I don't know," Brad admitted. "There were quite

a few people at Chad's that night, it was a casual sort of thing. People kept coming and going all through the evening. I've talked to a fair number of them and the stories, I have to admit, do tend to come on the same. Mike seemed tired but okay when he arrived. Later, though, he seemed very groggy. Maybe it was just plain exhaustion. He'd been working very hard, no doubt of that. Anyway, one of my friends did tell me he tried to get Mike to leave the party when he did but he couldn't budge him. He remembers that Chad said to leave Mike alone. He said he could stay there all night and sleep it off."

"And Susan Foster?"

"I talked to her myself later," Brad said soberly. "I'll admit she was vague, but I think this is because she was pretty high herself at the time. She doesn't seem to remember any words, any argument, nothing like that. She just remembers Michael firing the gun."

"It doesn't make sense," Karen insisted.

"It happened," he reminded her and sighed. "The waitress is sending out signals," he said then. "I think maybe we'd better order."

Brad scanned the oversize, red-clad menu and conversed with Karen about it, and they made decisions. Then, when the waitress had left them again, Brad said slowly, "There's no reason to think that Susan could have been mistaken, Karen. I only wish there were."

"Perhaps *she* shot Chad!" Karen ventured.

Brad shook his head. "She had no motive," he said flatly.

"Why not?"

"It was the first time she had ever met Chad," he told her. "Or Michael either, for that matter!"

Karen was incredulous. She said, "I thought Susan was Michael's girl at the time Chad was killed."

"No," Brad told her, shaking his head. "Your cousin was wrong about that. Michael had never met her until that night. The papers picked up on this business of her being his girl, evidently because it gave a kind of hearts-and-flowers touch. But it was completely inaccurate. Susan came to the party with two or three other nurses who *did* know Chad. She must have been enjoying herself because when they left she decided to stay longer, more's the pity, for her sake. That's what makes her story ring true. She had nothing to gain by lying."

"Do you know what happened to her after the trial?"

"As it happens, I do. I still keep in touch with another nurse who is a friend of hers. As I understand it, the experience of the trial was very rough on Susan. She was from New Hampshire, and she went back there once it was over. Not long after that, she married a fellow named Walter Petsky. They live in Nashua."

The dinner was delicious, but Karen had the feeling Brad wasn't appreciating the food any more than she was. Conversation lagged between them, and they both were silent on the drive back to Grand Isle.

The house was indigo, which meant that Maida still had not returned. Karen, wishing she had left a light on, said to Brad, "I'll go ahead, I know my way. You'll come in for a drink, won't you?"

Before he could answer her, lights flared in the living room, and an outside flood light beamed forth as the kitchen door was thrust open.

Karen's pulse began to pound. Despite Brad Simmons's comforting presence she could feel herself growing cold from fright's instinctive reaction as she halted in her tracks. Then Michael, his voice thick with anger, appeared in the kitchen doorway to call down to her, "Where the hell have you been?"

She sagged with relief. Then anger surged and she said accusingly, "You nearly scared the wits out of me!"

"Let's say it's mutual," he snapped back. "Dad tried to call you to ask if you'd come to our house for dinner. Finally he seemed so worried I told him I'd come over and check the place out. I—"

He broke off, as he saw Brad step out of his car.

"I see I was premature," he said coldly.

"Come on now," Brad Simmons protested. "Don't jump to conclusions, Mike!"

"That would hardly be necessary," Michael said and smiled an infuriating smile. Then, his lips twisting, he added with consummate irony, "After all, it's a free country, isn't it, *Doctor*?"

Before either of them could answer he turned and walked away, heading toward the steps that went down to the lakefront.

Karen, staring after him was speechless. Once again his attitude—to say nothing of his reactions—seemed inexplicable to her. And Brad, exhaling slowly, said, "Whew! He *is* touchy, isn't he! I can hardly blame him, though. If I'd been sitting here waiting for you...."

He looked down at her with an incipient expression

on his face which she was not inclined to cultivate further at the moment. She said hastily, "Brad, would you like a drink, or some coffee, before you go back to Burlington?"

"Thanks, but no," he said. "Our friend Michael might return, and something tells me he wouldn't welcome my presence."

She knew he was only teasing but nevertheless she said, "Don't be silly. Michael couldn't care less when you get down to facts." And she felt an odd little pang because she wished, more than anything, that this was not true.

It was cloudy Wednesday morning. Normally this might have caused Karen to sleep later than usual, but as it was she was thoroughly awake by six.

She checked Maida's room, hoping that her cousin had slipped in late last night. But she hadn't and this was worrisome. Maida *should* have been back by now, she told herself, and shortly before six thirty she was sufficiently concerned to dial Maida's Boston apartment. She was rewarded by a sleep-filled voice answering on the sixth ring.

Outraged, Maida said, "It's the middle of the night!"

"Not exactly," Karen said. "Why are you still there?"

"Because my former cold has turned into a sore throat, and the doctor has me on antibiotics," Maida said, being almost sullen about it. "For that matter, where have *you* been? I tried you any number of times last night."

"I went out to dinner."

"With Rod?"

"No. With a doctor I met in Burlington the other day."

"Well!"

"Don't start making a dramatic production out of it," Karen said quickly. "I was beginning to worry about you, that's why I called. I also wanted you to know, though, that I may be away most of today. I didn't want you to come back to an empty house."

"I'm going to stay here and suffer," Maida assured her, sounding rather sorry for herself. "You're not taking off for New York by any chance, are you, Karen?"

"No. I told you I'd wait on that. This is something else. I'll be back here by dinnertime."

She hung up before Maida could demand a further explanation. As she expected, the phone began jangling within seconds. She was sure it was Maida calling back with a barrage of questions, and she was not prepared to answer them!

She paused for coffee, then dressed, and, after making *sure* the doors were locked and the windows closed against possible rain, went out and started up her car.

She'd been right about her weather predictions. The rain started by the time she reached Burlington but Karen was not about to let anything deter her this morning. She picked up Interstate 89, driving diagonally across Vermont, paused for a late breakfast at White River Junction, and then was on into New Hampshire.

It was a magnificent road, and there was almost no traffic today. Despite the weather, the driving was easy, and Karen flexed her arm, pleased to find that it didn't ache nearly as much as it had only a week ago, when she had made her short, initial drive from Burlington to Grand Isle.

One week. Involvement. Again she remembered Hugh MacKnight's prescription for her, and knew now that if anyone had suggested to her a week ago how "involved" a person could become in the space of only seven days she would have been totally derisive.

She reached Nashua shortly before eleven o'clock, found a drug store with a pay phone, and scanned the directory. Her heart sank when she saw that there were seven Petskys listed. She thought of driving from address to address, then dismissed this as being purely impractical. She didn't know the city at all, so to make such a personal safari would waste valuable time. Instead, she changed a dollar into dimes and started phoning, asking each time she was answered, "Is this Susan?"

And, on the fourth ring, it was! Feeling quite proud of herself, Karen asked, "Susan Petoskey?"

"No," a soft voice responded, "Petsky."

"Sorry," Karen said. "I'm afraid I have the wrong person."

She hung up the receiver, her palms damp, her pulse beating fast. She was not used to practicing subterfuge, yet she had realized instinctively that it would not be wise to announce to Susan Petsky the fact that she was about to have a visitor. If there were anything to be gained from this interview, it must be done with an element of surprise.

Susan had already told her story on the witness

stand. Was there a chance that it might have been a prepared story? If so, the only way to hope to get her to change it was to catch her off guard, before she had a chance to slip back into rote.

Karen stopped at a filling station to get gas, and ask directions. Susan, she found, lived in a nondescript section of town, a neighborhood of old, double-decker houses that had seen better days. The name on a mailbox in a narrow, smelly vestibule revealed the fact that the Petsky flat was on the second floor. Karen dashed through the rain to the rear of the building, climbed steep steps, then pounded on a glass-paneled door given privacy by yellowed machine lace curtains.

There was such a long interval that she knocked again, afraid that she had perhaps not been so smart after all. The phone call very well may have aroused Susan Petsky's suspicions. Or, Karen conceded, possibly the girl had left home to do some late-morning errands.

She was on the verge of giving up when the door opened just a crack, and Karen found herself peering into enormous brown eyes that were not merely frightened, but terrified.

"Yes?" the girl asked, in the smallest of voices.

"Please," Karen said. "You don't know me, but I want to talk to you."

"Are you selling something?"

"No," Karen said. She swallowed hard. "This is about Chad Stanhope," she managed then.

The eyes grew larger, darker, and the thin face in which they dwelled paled visibly. Susan Petsky whispered, "Who are you?"

"Karen Morse, though that won't mean anything to you. But you see, I knew Chad, and I know Michael Stanhope, and—"

A man's voice cut in curtly. "Let her in!" he snapped.

Slowly Susan Petsky obeyed, edging the door open, letting Karen slip through what was little more than a crack.

She stepped over the threshold, then stopped short in astonishment. Her cousin Maida's husband, Jerry, stood facing her!

Jerry laughed shortly. "Believe me," he said, "you're no more surprised to see me than I am to see you!"

Jerry was tall, with rugged but handsome features, broad shoulders, and naturally wavy light brown hair. He reminded Karen faintly of Michael, but then she remembered that they were not blood relations, that this was coincidence, yet something that often happened in a family where there were adoptions. Jerry and Michael were, basically, of the same physical type, yet Michael was the taller of the two, and his good looks were considerably more arresting. Also there was a quiet strength to Michael that went beyond his obvious masculinity. He had been forged to steel, she found herself thinking, whereas though Jerry had known the sorrow of Chad's death—Chad, after all, *had* been his brother—he had not suffered in the same way at all.

Now, as she and Jerry stared disbelievingly at each other, Susan Petsky looked apprehensively first from one then to the other. She was a slight girl, in fact under ordinary circumstances she would have been too thin. Just now, however, the circumstances were not ordinary. Her stomach was startlingly distended. She was exceedingly pregnant; in fact, Karen felt sure, she must be close to the end of her term.

Her voice was almost querulous as she accosted Karen. "Who *are* you?" she demanded.

"Mr. Stanhope's cousin-in-law," Karen said, feeling more than a little inadequate.

"But why have you come *here*?" the girl persisted.

"Why, indeed, Karen?" Jerry Stanhope asked, an edge to his voice.

There was no point in evading the issue. Karen said, "I want to speak to Mrs. Petsky about the night Chad was killed."

"Then," Jerry said, "it would seem that we're here for the same reason!"

"Look," Susan Petsky said tightly, "I told my story on the witness stand. Now I want to *forget* it!"

She put her hands over her face, pressing her palms against her forehead. Karen glanced anxiously across at Jerry, and he frowned. She sensed that Jerry, experienced lawyer that he was, was having a hard time forming the questions he wanted to ask, and to her own surprise she took the initiative.

"Mrs. Petsky, you're the only witness to what happened. I think what we're both wondering is whether there may not be something you've remembered after all this time. Something you overlooked in the horror of the moment."

Karen found herself staring into tormented brown eyes, but even as she witnessed their pain she felt a stab of triumph. There was something about the girl's expression that made her virtually certain Susan Petsky *did* know something, and she held her breath, waiting to hear it.

But instead Susan swayed and shook her head. "You can't imagine!" Then she caught her breath. She cried out, "Oh!" and it was a high pitched, strained little word. "Oh, dear *God*!" Then, like a rag doll falling from a shelf, she crumpled to the floor at Jerry's feet.

Jerry, ashen faced, picked her up and carried her to a sagging old couch, covered with a cheap, foam-back tan throw. Karen ran into a bathroom where the plumbing was of a decidedly earlier vintage, found a washcloth, dipped it in cold water, then ran back and began bathing the girl's face.

Susan, rallying, said weakly, "My labor's begun."

This, Karen decided wryly, must surely be one of fate's more capricious whims. "Who is your doctor, Susan?" she asked quickly.

"Dr. LeFevre," the girl said. "His number's on the pad, over by the phone. I saw him yesterday. He said it could be any time—"

Karen looked up and met Jerry's eyes. "I'll take her to the hospital," she said, and he nodded.

She found the doctor's phone number and dialed, then spoke to the doctor with a calm that she couldn't quite believe. Yes, she told him, she had a car. Yes, she would bring Susan in immediately.

Susan said weakly, "My bag's all packed. It's right inside the bedroom closet. Look, someone's got to call Walter."

Walter. Karen remembered the name in the telephone book. Walter Petsky. She said, "We'll call Walter, Susan. Right now, though, we've got to take care of you."

She found the bag, and took a shapeless raincoat down from a closet hook. Jerry helped Susan to her feet, and they walked her down a flight of stairs and then out into the drizzle, helping her struggle into the front seat of the compact.

Jerry said, "Karen, come back here when you can, will you? I'll wait."

Starting the car, Karen nodded, absorbed for the moment in other things. "Susan, you'll have to give me directions."

"You go straight ahead for three blocks, then you turn right," Susan said. "I'll tell you when we get near." She leaned back, sighed deeply. "Look," she said, "don't forget to call Walter, will you? He works at Farrington Mills. Their number is in the book."

"I won't forget." Karen promised again.

"Turn right at the next corner," she directed.

It was incredible. This couldn't be happening. Karen told herself this as she made the turn, then glanced at the girl by her side. Susan's face was waxen, and her forehead became beaded in sweat as another pain gripped her. It was, of course, impossible to ask her anything at all about the night Chad died, but still the frustration was overwhelming.

As she pulled up at the hospital's emergency entrance, Karen told herself there would have to be another trip to Nashua when Susan *could* talk.

Involved!

As she went inside the hospital to get help, Karen winced at the mere thought of the word.

Chapter Eleven

They sat at a booth in a diner on the outskirts of town, facing each other across a chipped red plastic-topped table. A waitress put mugs of steaming coffee in front of them and added a hamburger for Jerry.

Jerry looked at it without appetite, then said, "You should eat something too. You look done in."

"I am, emotionally," Karen admitted. "Right now, though, I think if I ate anything it would make me sick."

"You may have something there," he conceded. He looked across at her unhappily. "How's Maida?"

"As miserable as you are," Karen said, without even pausing to weigh words.

Jerry's eyebrows tilted upward, and again she was reminded of Michael. He said tightly, "I understand she's been in Boston, seeing her lawyer."

"The legal fraternity must have quite a grapevine," Karen observed wryly.

"Touché." He rumpled his hair, and said dully, "It all goes back to the business about Chad, Karen. The whole thing has—well, it has eaten at me ever since. That's why I tracked down Susan Petsky. I know it's wishful thinking, but I keep praying that she'll suddenly remember something that will prove Michael didn't kill my brother. I don't seem to be able to live with the thought of that."

Karen stared at him. "Somehow," she said, "I had the impression you had no doubts about Michael's guilt. In fact, I had an idea you—well, that you've hated him, ever since it happened."

He didn't answer her directly. First he said with a faint, wry smile, "You're on a first-name basis with him, I see. How did that come to pass? I don't recall your ever having met."

Karen flushed. "I've been at Grand Isle with Maida," she said. "He's there, at his father's house."

"Yes," Jerry said. "I know. We keep in touch."

"But I thought—"

He shook his head gently. "You're right about Michael and myself, to a point, Karen. At the trial I hated him so violently I think I could have killed him with my own hands. When Susan took the stand to give her testimony, I couldn't look at him!"

He continued, his voice husky, "Later, after Michael had gone to prison, Uncle Doug called me one day and told me Michael wanted to see me. I couldn't face up to that, though. I refused to visit him. Then Aunt Eleanor died. Michael was at the funeral—with a prison guard, of course, although they tried to be as inconspicuous as possible about that out of consideration for Uncle Doug. Michael looked so ghastly it was hard even for me not to feel some compassion for him. Then there was Uncle Doug's accident."

"How did it happen?"

"He was on his way to court one morning. It was

early, we'd had an ice storm and the roads were bad. He skidded—" Jerry sighed. "He was in the hospital for weeks. I visited him often, but we never mentioned Michael. I sensed he wanted to talk about him, but I didn't. Finally Uncle Doug was strong enough to go up to Grand Isle with Horace—"

"Who *is* Horace?"

"A man whom Uncle Doug befriended, redeemed, I guess you could say. He was headed straight for skid row, but somehow Uncle Doug managed to reach out to him. Uncle Doug has a way with people, as I'm sure you've found out for yourself. Anyway, Horace saw a story in the paper about the accident, and he went to see Uncle Doug in the hospital. He told him he wanted to be with him for as long as Uncle Doug needed him, for the rest of his life, as far as he was concerned. He went and took nursing courses, therapy courses; he did everything he possibly could do so that he would be of real value to Uncle Doug."

"He must have taken cooking courses too."

Jerry smiled. "No. That's what he was, among other things. A professional chef as well as a professional wrestler!"

He pushed his unfinished hamburger aside and said, "Anyway, Uncle Doug went to Grand Isle with Horace and then last year in November, just before Thanksgiving, Michael was paroled. I knew he was going to be paroled, but it never occurred to me that he would seek me out. However, the afternoon after he was released, he walked right into my office. I doubt if anything or anyone could have stopped him. My secretary came trailing behind him, half scared to death, apologizing. I told her to leave us alone. Michael stood in front of my desk, and he looked about a hundred feet tall and as if someone had carved him out of solid granite. Then he took a gun out of his overcoat pocket—"

"A *gun*?"

Jerry nodded. "Yes. I never did ask him where he got it. We both knew he was in total violation of his parole to have it on him at all. I imagine, actually, that he asked someone he'd met in prison about where he could get a gun, and he followed through as quickly as possible."

Karen, shaken, said, "Are you saying that he threatened you with this gun, Jerry?"

"God, no," Jerry said simply. "He put it down on the desk in front of me, and he said, 'Go ahead and use it. It can't be traced. Or, if you rather, I'll use it on myself. If I killed Chad, I deserve to die.'"

"*If* he killed Chad?"

"Yes. He had been in mental agony for three years in prison. You've seen him. True, you didn't know him before, but even so you must be aware of the mark it's left on him. His hair even turned gray.

"He told me that during those three years he had more than enough time to think, and he went over every second of that terrible night—or as much of it as he could remember—again and again and again. He had been working very hard at the hospital, and that night when he went to Chad he'd had almost no sleep for much too long a time. He said he wouldn't have gone at all, but he'd gotten some extra liquor for Chad and felt that he should hold to his promise of taking it over. He intended to stay only briefly, but he had a couple of quick drinks, and they really hit him."

"He remembers that?"

"Yes. He remembers everything quite clearly, to a certain point. Then he says that it's as if a curtain fell, shutting everything out. Looking back, he thinks it must have been the coffee."

"The *coffee*?"

"Yes. After the second drink, he decided to get a cup of coffee, to wake himself up. He says Chad usually kept a pot going on the back of the stove, but it was empty. One of the nurses at the party was in the kitchen, though, and she said she'd brew up a cup of instant for him."

"Susan?"

"No. A girl named Betty. Susan had come to the party with her."

"Did Michael drink the coffee?"

"Yes, he did. This girl, Betty, came into the living room after a time and told him she'd brewed up a couple of cups for him in a small pot. He went out and got it; he remembers pouring the coffee into a mug and he says he took it black, no cream, no sugar. Shortly afterward, everything went bleary. He went into the living room and sat down in an armchair, and he thinks he actually passed out for a while. Then he remembers seeing swirls of bright colors and hearing voices, but there was nothing clear. When things finally did become clear again, the police were there. Chad was lying on the floor, and Susan was over in the corner, crying."

"Who called the police?"

"Susan. She said there were only the three of them there when it happened. Chad, Michael, and herself."

"So," Karen said softly, "if there *is* any sort of key, it is Susan who holds it."

"So it would seem," Jerry admitted. "But Michael and I had a transcript made of the trial, we've gone over it so many times we could each quote every word of the testimony by memory, and there doesn't seem to be any loophole."

There was pain in Jerry's eyes now as he said, "It looks as if Michael and I will have to live with the facts as they were presented, both of us. Yet, I keep hoping against hope. That," he added bitterly, "is why I finally decided to come up here and talk to her myself...for all the good it's done!"

The drive back to Grand Isle was punctuated with intermittent rain showers, and Karen, tired now, had to concentrate on her driving to the point where there wasn't time to dwell on the highly unexpected meeting with Jerry.

Jerry had looked bitterly weary as they walked to their respective cars, and she had felt a surge of sympathy for him, tinged with annoyance at both him and Maida. There was enough trouble in the world, she thought, without two people who so obviously loved each other refusing to come back together because of pride, stubbornness, or whatever one wished to call it.

It was nearly dark when she reached Grand Isle, and she was afraid that the Barnes's store would be closed, but fortunately the lights were still on. Karen bought milk and eggs and a loaf of bread, then added a can of hash, which would do for supper for both of them if Maida was back.

There were other customers in the store, so she had no chance for conversation with Roger Barnes. But as she left, a small figure came around the side of the building, heading toward her. Ambrose.

The rain had stopped, at least temporarily, but he still wore a yellow slicker. "Hey, Karen," he said, and smiled his engaging, freckle-faced, heart-stopping grin. "Want to give me a ride? I'm going down to Mike's."

"I'd be glad to," she agreed.

"Here," he said, "I'll carry your groceries for you."

She gave him the brown paper bag and he trundled beside her out to the car. Once they were settled in, he said, "Mike's going to help me with my math."

"Oh?"

"He's pretty good at it," Ambrose said solemnly. "He tries to make it kind of like a game. I'm still not too keen on it, though."

"I'm not too keen on it either," she admitted, "but it's still worth learning. It's something you use all your life, so the better you are at it the easier a lot of things become for you."

"I guess so," Ambrose conceded doubtfully.

As they neared the fork in the road, Ambrose said, "It was fun, having you come fishing the other day. I think Mike liked it a lot." His voice became conspiratorial. "Can you keep a secret?"

"I think so."

"Okay. I'll tell you something I haven't even told Mike. One of these times I'm going over and spend the night out on the island."

"Not by yourself!" she protested.

Ambrose grinned. "Why not? I'm old enough." He considered the matter, then added practically, "I think I'll wait a while, though, till it gets warmer than it is now."

"You'd better wait *quite* a while!" she told him pointedly.

They were nearing the house, and she saw Maida's car parked at the side. Relieved, she said, "My cousin's back. Look, Ambrose, if you'll wait just a minute I'll run in with the groceries and say hello to her. Then I'll drive you around."

"I can walk on across."

She shook her head. "It's starting to rain again. There's no point to your getting soaked."

She carried the groceries into the kitchen, calling out Maida's name, but there was no answer. Then she saw the note by the phone, written in Maida's distinctive, curved hand.

"You've had two phone calls," it read. "Dr. Hugh MacKnight and Dr. Bradley Simmons. And *I've* had a phone call from Jerry! I've gone over to Uncle Doug's to give him a message. Come on over."

Karen smiled. It hadn't taken Jerry long to come to a decision in regard to Maida after all!

She went back to the car to find Ambrose sitting behind the steering wheel.

"Another couple of years, and I'll be driving myself," he told her, then slid across into the passenger seat.

Michael's orange car was parked at the end of the crescent driveway, and she pulled up next to it. Horace, answering the door, said, "Everyone's in the library, miss. Ambrose, I've got some brownies for you out in the kitchen."

As Ambrose happily followed Horace, Karen stood

for a hesitant moment in the foyer. Then slowly she crossed the living room, with its grand piano in the corner, and went on into the library.

Maida was sitting in an armchair, and the judge had pulled up his wheelchair directly across from her. Karen's eyes touched upon both of them, and then she felt her pulse begin to throb with such force that she thought its thrust surely must be visible.

Michael was in front of the fireplace, putting another log on a fire that was becoming well established. He turned to face her, ostensibly as inscrutable as ever and yet she would have sworn that there was a light in those peridot eyes that had very little to do with a reflection from the blaze on the hearth.

"Hello, Karen," he said, and she at once found herself voiceless. Why couldn't she get a better grip on herself where this man was concerned?

He was wearing faded jeans again, but tonight his knit shirt was a vivid shade of red that set off his unusual coloring and made her much too aware of the latent strength that seemed to emanate from him. And she was aware too of the proud thrust of his head and that defiance that was so very hard to brook.

"Well," Maida said, "so my wandering cousin has returned! Where *have* you been, darling? Judging from your phone messages, I'd say you've been involved in some sort of medical convention!"

She couldn't look at Michael, and she was relieved when the judge said, "Mike, will you do the honors and get Karen a drink? And you might refill ours, while you're at it."

"I'll help," she said quickly.

As they walked down the hallway, she was distressingly conscious of him. He towered over her, and she nearly stumbled over her own feet in her effort to match his stride. Either he was unaware of this or, more likely, he simply didn't care about it, she concluded, and knew, sickeningly, that the wall was up again. He seemed, in fact, more aloof than ever, his clear-cut profile averted.

She said tentatively, "Ambrose drove over with me."

"Oh?"

"I picked him up at the store. He said you're going to help him with his math."

"That's right."

"Michael..."

"Yes?"

"Nothing."

They reached the kitchen, and to her surprise there was no one in it. She looked up at Michael inquiringly, and he said, "Horace and Ambrose have probably gone up to my room. We usually work up there. Horace will keep him amused until I get there."

Horace kept the major part of the liquor supply in a corner cabinet, and turning to it, Michael asked, "What would you like?"

He spoke so abruptly that she stiffened and automatically tilted her chin upward. "Look," she said, matching his coldness, "go on up to Ambrose if you want to. If you'll tell me what the others have been having, I can make the drinks."

He shook his head. "Not until I've had a word or two with you," he told her, and there was an iciness to his clear green eyes that made her flinch.

"About what?" she managed to ask, then added

bitterly, "Do you mean that we actually may have something to talk about?"

"Yes," he said steadily. "Yes, I think we do indeed have something to talk about. How did you happen to be with Brad Simmons last night?"

"I had dinner with him," she said defiantly.

"And how did *that* happen?"

She flushed, despite herself, but she said levelly, "I don't think that's any of your concern."

"On the contrary," he told her, "I think it's very much my concern."

"Then you think wrong."

She turned away from him, but in an instant he gripped her shoulders, twisting her so that she was forced to face him.

"Damn it, Karen," he said, his voice low, his tone menacing, "get out of my business and stay out of it, will you! I called Brad Simmons today and asked him how the two of you happened to be together, and he told me you'd phoned him and asked him to meet you. He was delighted, needless to say. Who wouldn't be?"

"Oh?"

"Don't try to be arch!" he snapped. "Flirt with anyone else you want to flirt with, but don't try it with me. I don't need it. And how many times do I have to tell you I don't need *you?* I don't *want* you in my business, so get out of it! Do you understand what I'm saying?"

She stared up at him, despising her own weakness because she was afraid she couldn't hold back the tears. It seemed to her that he was watching her in disgust, and she suspected that he viewed tears as a purely feminine weapon for which he had very little use. She was waging a fight to suppress them, though, and it was such an obvious one that she saw the green eyes darken and an expression she couldn't translate creep into them. He was still gripping her shoulders but now the pressure lightened, and she knew that in another moment she would be in his arms. Again she despised herself for her weakness because she could not wait to feel the pressure of his lips on hers and to know the pure, transcending, sensual joy of his kiss.

But this was not to be. "Mike," a small voice said, and they both swung around. Ambrose stood in the doorway, trying to look as if he had been neither watching nor listening.

"What is it, Ambrose?" Michael asked evenly.

"I got to get home by eight o'clock," Ambrose said, "which doesn't give us much time."

"Right." Michael nodded. "I'll be along as soon as I make some drinks for people."

"Could I maybe have a Coke?" Ambrose suggested.

"Yes," Michael said. "Run along and I'll bring it up to you."

Ambrose left them, lagging only slightly, and Michael actually smiled. Smiles often transformed faces, Karen conceded, but she didn't think she'd ever before noted such a change as that which came over Michael when, even momentarily, he lowered his guard.

He said, the smile turning into a rueful grin that was a heart-tugger, "Ambrose does seem to burst in on us as if he's been programmed to interrupt at high-tension moments." And, miraculously, Karen found herself relaxing.

Michael had moved away from her with Ambrose's entrance. Now he reached out to cup her chin in his strong, slender hand.

"It looks as if *I've* been programmed to apologize to you at regular intervals," he told her, still rueful. "Too frequently, I'd say, but here it goes again. I'm sorry, Karen. I admit I get into too much depth about things. I still find myself tensing up over trifles, much more than I should. Be patient with me, will you?"

It was a totally unexpected question, one which Karen was not prepared to answer because, again, words eluded her. As she stared up at him, there was so much she wanted to say. She wanted to tell him that she was ready to be patient forever—if, that is, there was truth to the old cliché that patience brought its own reward. In this case, the reward would be his love.

At the thought of this—at the thought of ever sharing even a portion of his love—Karen became transfused by a feeling so poignant in its sweetness that she could feel the tears threatening again, and this time she really fought to keep them back. She couldn't let him see her cry again!

She said, her voice unsteady despite her efforts, "Of course I'll be patient with you."

His kiss was brief, but the tenderness of it had a telling effect. She was rocked emotionally as he stepped back again, and this time the smile that flickered across his face was entirely too elusive.

"I'd better get the drinks ready or it'll be a long day before my father asks me to bartend again," he said casually. "What's your pleasure?"

"A glass of white wine, please," she told him, and he nodded.

"As the lady wishes," he said gravely, and set about the task of putting the drinks together.

As she stood watching him, there was no doubt in Karen's mind at all that there had been a double-edged meaning to his question about her preferences.

What should she have said? "*You're* what the lady wishes, Michael"?

Now, as he took out ice cubes and clinked them into waiting glasses, she could only wonder what his reaction would have been!

Michael carried the tray of drinks back to the library and then excused himself, explaining that he had promised to help Ambrose with his studies.

The judge, looking after him as he left, said, "Michael spends a lot of time with that boy, but it's good for both of them. Karen, Maida hasn't had the chance to tell you some really wonderful news. Jerry is coming up here tomorrow!"

Karen had no need to simulate surprise. She hadn't expected such quick action on Jerry's part.

"Yes," Maida said. "He wants to get away from the rest of the world for a few days. He told me to tell Michael he hopes they can do some fishing together."

The judge chuckled. "Ambrose will probably insist upon making it a threesome," he prophesied. He turned his attention to Karen. "My dear," he said, "I don't want you to feel that I imagine I have a claim on your time. I *was* worried when you didn't show up today. But I might have assumed that you had merely other things to do if it hadn't been for Michael. He came in every ten minutes to see if you were here."

Maida said lightly, "She's dangerous, Uncle Doug. Every man she meets—"

"Oh, stop it, Maida!" Karen snapped swiftly.

Maida looked hurt, and the judge said smoothly, "Anyone would know you two are related. You're both charmers!"

With this he switched to other subjects, but Karen only half heard what he was saying.

Michael had been the one who'd been concerned about her yesterday! Her thoughts whirled as she considered the implications about this, then she warned herself that she must not read too much meaning to it, or to Michael's reactions about her going out with Brad Simmons. In retrospect, they seemed to hold their quota of something that seemed very much like jealousy. But here too, she told herself, she must not leap to conclusions.

Horace came in to suggest refills, but Maida, glancing at her watch, shook her head. "I promised June we'd come over for a bowl of her real Texas chili," she said.

Karen had no particular desire to sample June's chili at the moment, but no gracious excuse to escape this commitment came to mind. So she left with Maida after assuring the judge that she would be over to resume their work in the morning.

June Kensington wore a caftan that was an exotic blend of orange and yellow and lime green, with gold slippers on her slender feet and dangling gold and jade drops at her ears. She *was* striking, that Karen had to concede.

They had daiquiris followed by chili, hot enough to

bring tears to one's eyes but delicious. Next came chocolate ice cream, sprinkled with cinnamon. "To slake the fires," June said.

Rod monitored the stereo, which provided pleasant music. They let the sound wash over them, and the conversation was variable enough to be interesting. It was, in all, a pleasant and reasonably relaxing evening, and it was not until she was getting ready for bed that Karen realized Michael's name had not been mentioned once, nor had Maida revealed to the Kensingtons that Jerry would be arriving the following day.

The judge was already at work when Karen presented herself at the big spruce-colored house the following morning. Horace brought in coffee and sweet rolls and she told him in mock despair that if he didn't stop feeding her she'd be getting fat. This actually elicited from him what passed as a rusty smile.

She settled down at the typewriter and soon became absorbed in the judge's notes. This was a fascinating subject to her, an echo of her own childhood in a way, and as she read and typed the time passed quickly. She became lost in another world, to be brought back to the present only when she heard Michael's voice.

"I don't think I'd want to work for you, Dad!" he said. "Don't you even give the help time out to eat?"

Karen and the judge looked up at him simultaneously, their faces wearing almost identical blank, abstracted expressions. Michael laughed. "Horace asked me to tell you that lunch is ready," he informed them.

So he was joining them today! Karen, trying to conceal her elation at the mere thought of this, excused herself long enough to make a trip to the bathroom. She combed her hair, touched up her lipstick, and even daubed on some cologne from a purse-size vial, and could not help but notice that, as she did so, her fingers were trembling. And this was a tremor that had absolutely nothing to do with her bad arm.

Michael held her chair for her once she'd arrived in the dining room, and then sat down opposite her. The judge dominated the place at the head of the table and he also dominated the conversation, which was as well, for Karen never before had felt so tongue-tied.

Lunch over, Michael asked, "Dad, could you spare Karen for a while? I told Horace I'd run out to La-Porte's farm to get some fresh eggs, and I thought she might like to come along."

The judge scowled. "You *do* think I'm a slave driver, don't you!" he protested in mock anger. Then he darted a quick glance of pleasure in Karen's direction, and she knew she was trapped.

Michael was almost courtly as he held the car door for her. She got in, feeling like an abashed schoolgirl. They started up the road, and he said, "I hope you don't mind my doing this. I had to get you away from the house so I could talk to you."

The light green eyes swept her face. He said levelly, "I did a lot of thinking last night. You were right, of course. The fact that you went out to dinner with Brad Simmons was, essentially, none of my business. The only thing that makes it my business is that evidently you got in touch with him in the first place to ask him about Susan."

Karen gave a start of surprise, but before she could speak Michael went on to say, "Jerry called me last night after you'd left. We've been in touch for a long while. Matter of fact, I've been keeping an eye on the place up here for him and evidently frightened Maida half to death her first night here when I thought she was an intruder and she thought I was one!

"Anyway, last night Jerry told me about meeting you in Nashua." He drew a long breath, then exhaled it very slowly. "Just what do you think you were doing?" he demanded. "It's enough to have Jerry take off on a damned fool wild goose chase, but why should *you*—"

She was clenching her hands, because now they were really shaking. In fact, she felt as if everything within her was coming close to the shattering point.

Michael continued, without waiting for an answer. "Don't you think I've already exhausted every possibility there was to exhaust? I've gone over everything there was to go over again and again and again. Believe me, your prying is only going to make matters a great deal worse and I'm warning you now to stop it! This is absolutely none of your business, as I've already told you several times, including last night. But what I said last night goes threefold now. I hadn't talked to Jerry then."

Despite himself, his voice shook slightly. And glancing across at him, Karen saw that he was gripping the steering wheel so tightly his knuckles were white.

"Why *did* you do this?" he demanded tautly.

She stared straight ahead, unseeingly. She yearned to say, I looked at you and there was something about you that cried out to me. I sensed something in you that provoked a response I've never felt before, and when you kissed me....

She wanted to say, I've fallen in love with you. But she could imagine how he would scoff at her, even if she were to come close to such a confession.

She thought of Hugh MacKnight's word, and she used it. She said lamely, "I—I just seemed to become involved."

His voice was caustic. "Involved? That makes you sound like a frustrated social worker!"

"I certainly didn't mean it that way!"

"Well, then, what did you mean? What are you, Karen? Merely champion of the underdog and crusader for justice?" His sarcasm was a slashing thing, each word like a cutting sliver of ice.

Karen was coming to the end of her emotional rope. The tension between them was so intense that she felt as if her mind, her feelings, had been blown to the breaking point. Her pulse pounded, and the gamut of feelings she was experiencing seemed to have gone beyond her capacity to cope.

She clapped her hands over her ears, and nearly shrieked the words. "Stop it, Michael!"

"Why should I stop it?" he asked her coldly. "I've had more than my fill of being a case history." He was staring straight ahead now, and though he was apparently devoting his entire concentration to the road ahead of him his voice was constricted. "Look, I don't deny that I find you attractive physically—very attractive. You already know that. It's pretty clear that there've been moments when neither of us has been able to keep our hands off each other. But that's a matter of body chemistry, Karen. I would be less than human if I didn't respond to you in that sense. I was a long time without women, you may remember."

She glared at him. "You make me sound like some kind of animal!"

His laugh was short. He said, "There's more than a touch of animal in most of us, wouldn't you say? However, as far as women in my life are concerned, that compartment has been taken care of, and you might as well know it."

June. If the compartment in his life involving a woman was "taken care of," then it must be June with whom he intended to share whatever was ahead of him. June who clearly had been a part of his past, was now also to become a part of his future.

"I don't mean to be callous, though it probably seems that way," Michael said. "I just think you should know you're wasting your time in your efforts to 'rehabilitate' me. You're wasting your time here on Grand Isle, for that matter. Jerry's due back today—"

"So," Karen said, finding her voice finally and cutting in on him, "what you are saying is that it's time for me to leave. Right?"

"I should think so."

"What about my work with your father?"

He shrugged. "I don't deny that he finds your company pleasant," he admitted. "But he has the rest of his life in which to work on this project, after all. He's in no hurry. He enjoys puttering alone among my mother's things. Evidently Maida told him something about your surgeon in New York suggesting that you become involved in something, for the sake of therapy, and my father's a great one for helping people out."

"In other words," she said, stung, "what you're

saying is that he invented the job for me because of *me*, not because he really needed help?''

''Wouldn't it seem so?''

She was hurt by this to the point of physical pain. The judge had been the one really bright note in a world too often gray since she'd come to Grand Isle. He had given her not only a feeling of being needed but a sense of real rapport, as well, that had been very warming. Now Michael was saying that he had acted toward her only out of sympathy.

She subsided into silence, fighting emotions that had become chaotic. Bruised, she felt a surge of hate toward this man at her side. Michael had said he didn't mean to be callous, but this she didn't believe. It seemed to her, rather, that he was doing everything he could to ride roughshod over her feelings.

Again she asked herself why.

They came to the farm, and Karen stayed in the car, huddled into the corner of the front seat, while Michael got out to exchange pleasantries with the ruddy-faced, smiling French Canadian farmer. He brought back eggs, plus a gallon of maple syrup, putting his purchases in the backseat without comment.

She had no wish for further conversation on the way home, nor did he attempt any. He turned on the radio, setting the volume high enough so that waltz music engulfed them. Talking was effectively blocked.

Once they'd pulled up in front of the house she left him without a further word and tried to fight off an intense feeling of despondency as she went back to the workroom. It was a fruitless attempt, though. She could only hope she didn't look as miserable as she felt.

The judge had unearthed a sheaf of his wife's notes dealing with her collection, these to be incorporated with notes he had made himself. Karen started correlating the information, and it proved to be slow work. By the middle of the afternoon she had developed such a headache that she asked the judge to excuse her, and she went back to Maida's, took some aspirin, and fell asleep.

She awoke to hear voices in the living room. A man and a woman. She heard Maida laugh, and there was such happiness in the laugh she knew Jerry had come back.

Michael was right. It *was* time for her to leave Grand Isle, despite the fact that so much was still unresolved. If she stayed, she would be playing the role of third person on a second honeymoon, and she didn't look forward to this.

Although she had had her full share of bad moments since the plane crash that had marked such a turning point in her life, she never before had felt quite so alone.

Chapter Twelve

It was bright and beautiful on Friday. Jerry, dressed in an old plaid shirt and well-worn jeans, seemed thoroughly content to putter around, looking over both his fishing tackle and his old rowboat.

Late in the morning Brad Simmons called to ask if Karen would have dinner with him that night. She was not relishing the prospect of being the third at Jerry and Maida's dinner table, so she quickly said yes. She had barely hung up the receiver when the judge called for Maida, saying that he had invited Rod and June Kensington for dinner and hoped Jerry, Maida, and Karen would come to round out the party.

"Karen has a dinner date," Maida said airily, "but we'd love to join you."

For a bitter moment Karen wished that she had not been so quick to accept Brad. Then she told herself it was as well that she had. Tonight's party would be a family affair. For although Michael was not related by blood he was surely a part of the clan. He had been a Stanhope most of his life.

Karen had realized on awakening this morning that

she could not possibly face another meeting with Michael until she'd gained far more control of her senses than she possessed now. These past few days especially he had kept her on an emotional seesaw, and she'd lost all sense of equilibrium when it came to getting back into anything approaching a normal frame of mind.

He had been cruel yesterday afternoon, though. It had been one thing to try again to convince her that she had no role to play in his life, even to indicate that there was someone else with whom he was involved—and it seemed to her that it almost had to be June—but it had been insulting to say that everything that had been between them could be put down to "body chemistry." She'd felt like something out of a test tube.

A microbe, she thought angrily. Just so much bacteria!

Also it was a matter of deep chagrin to think that she had imagined Michael might actually have been jealous of Brad Simmons where she was concerned. What Michael had resented, she knew very well now, was not her going out with the young doctor but the fact that he had considered she'd been "prying"—that was his word for it—into his affairs. There had been no chance, under the circumstances, to even begin to convince him that this was not mere curiosity on her part, nor was she the do-gooder he had so bitterly accused her of being. She could not explain fully even to herself why it had become so burningly important to her to see Michael vindicated. But even now, even now when he'd made serious dents in the self-confidence she was just beginning to get a grip on, she knew that she'd do a great deal to see his name cleared.

Nothing could ever be right for Michael Stanhope again until the cloud that hung over him—a cloud of guilt—had somehow been dissipated. Yet he seemed so sure that this could never happen.

A terrible thought crossed her mind. Was it possible that Michael remembered more of that awful night when Chad had been killed than he had ever admitted? Was it possible that the events of that night were not so hazy to him after all?

Could he be guilty?

Still lying on her bed with the sunlight streaming through her window, Karen actually had shaken her head firmly when she got to this. She was as sure, as sure as she was that she was alive, that Michael was innocent.

Misguided faith, perhaps? She supposed that a lot of people would say that was what it was. But she didn't think so.

Nevertheless it had been wrong of him to make her think that the judge had asked her to help him in his work only as a kind of panacea, an aid to her therapy, and not because he had needed her. This certainly hadn't seemed to be the case yesterday when she'd returned to work with him until the headache had stopped her. The judge had appeared to be very grateful, and she couldn't believe that this was all pretense on his part.

This morning she'd gotten up, after all this speculation, intending to go across to the big house after she'd had some breakfast. She had, in fact, even started out, planning first to take the shortcut through

the woods, then changing her mind and starting down
the road toward the fork, instead.

Well before she reached the fork, though, she'd
changed her mind again. The idea of letting the judge
down—if, in fact, that was what she was doing—did
give her a nagging sense of guilt. But the risk of meeting Michael was too great. This morning she could not
face those peridot eyes.

He had not come near the workroom yesterday afternoon after she'd left the car while he was still sitting in it. Now she wondered how he must feel about
her having been invited to dinner tonight? There was
a chance that he might sidestep dinner himself if it
meant having to be in her presence. And that would
be needless, because she'd be with Brad and, dammit,
she was going to enjoy herself. Her chin tilted upward
as she told herself this firmly.

Along the way, before reaching the fork, she found
a path that cut through the woods in an opposite direction and she followed it, reveling in the peace, the
verdant foliage, and the tangy, clean scent of the
pines. She'd always loved this particular fragrance.
Now it reminded her of Michael. The pines, the lake,
Michael, somehow they all belonged together. They
would always be pictured together in her mind.

I will never forget him, she thought disconsolately as
she wandered along.

At length she came out to a cliff overlooking the
lake. She clambered down it, then slowly wandered
back to the farmhouse along the lakefront to find that
Maida had joined Jerry and was perched on top of one
of the big boulders, talking to him. Watching them, it
seemed impossible to Karen that the two of them had

ever even contemplated divorce. They so obviously belonged together.

This realization too spurred a sense of loneliness so intense that she knew action was the only possible course to follow at the moment unless she were going to bog down into a veritable mire of self-pity. So she drove to Ambrose's father's store and bought the makings for a lavish salad, which she prepared for lunch for Jerry, Maida, and herself.

After lunch she took a nap, then lingered over dressing for her date with Brad. She wanted to look especially good tonight if only to prove to herself that she could do so.

She chose to wear a deceptively simple topaz silk dress that highlighted her eyes and had the plus of clinging in precisely the right places. Then she brushed her hair until it shone, added antique topaz earrings, and a splash of L'Air du Temps.

Having taken all the time she could over these preparations, she stared for a long time at her reflection in the mirror. Astonishingly she really looked herself again for the first time since the crash. The only obvious difference was the edge of maturity her long ordeal had given her, and actually this had brought with it an added measure of beauty. Karen could take note of this objectively, for there was no conceit in her where either her appearance or her musical ability was concerned. She knew that she looked lovelier right now than she had for a very long while. But there was no satisfaction to this realization at all.

There would never be any satisfaction in being beautiful... unless it was for Michael, she thought bleakly.

Maida was still dressing for her own dinner date when Brad Simmons arrived, but Jerry was in the living room, scanning a magazine. Karen introduced the two men and Jerry was pleasant enough—his good manners never seemed to fail him—yet she detected an expression in his eyes she couldn't quite define. Annoyance? Surprise? Disapproval? She chided herself for being imaginative. Certainly there was no reason why Jerry should disapprove of Brad!

Brad took her to a charming place near Highgate Springs where the food was delicious, and there was a small combo for dancing. And she could not help but enjoy being with him. He was excellent company, obviously relishing this off-duty night, and there was comfort, if not excitement, to the strength of his arms encircling her as they danced.

It was slightly after eleven when they got back to Grand Isle, Brad having said reluctantly that he had to be on duty at six the next morning, and so couldn't make as much of a night of it as he would have liked.

"Maybe next weekend, if I could wangle the time off, we could go up to Montreal," he suggested. "It's a fantastic city."

"So I've heard." She smiled. Admittedly, she knew, it would be fun to go to Montreal with Brad Simmons, but there were other things to be faced.

"I probably won't be here next weekend, Brad," she said slowly. "I'll have to be getting back to New York shortly."

"No!" His disappointment was keen. "Somehow," he told her, "I had the idea you'd be staying around a while."

She shook her head, trying to be light about it. "No, my cousin's husband is here now. So there's really no reason to stay any longer."

He grinned ruefully. "I'd like to think I could be something of a reason, Karen."

"Brad..."

"I know," he told her quickly. "What about Mike, Karen?"

She flushed. "Michael... doesn't really enter into this," she said stiffly.

"I'd like to think that was true," he admitted, and perhaps because she wanted to prove to herself that it *was* true she let him hold her tightly, let him kiss her, and felt herself responding to a point, only because he was both attractive and a very nice person. But she experienced none of the rapture that always came when Michael kissed her. Nor would she ever, with anyone else, she thought sadly.

Karen knew she was not being fair to either Brad or herself by encouraging him. Yet when he said "I'll call you tomorrow," she nodded assent.

Maida and Jerry came home a few minutes later, and Karen noted an odd expression in Jerry's eyes when he saw her. Relief?

"Uncle Doug told me to tell you he missed you, both tonight and today, as well," Maida said. "He thought you'd be along to do some work with him. He's grown very fond of you, Karen."

Karen blinked back tears and said unsteadily, "He's a dear person."

Jerry looked at her curiously, but he didn't comment, and Maida didn't seem to notice. Yawning, she said, "It was a fun evening, except that June is so obvious about Michael. I wish she'd keep her hands off him."

"It's up to Michael to keep them off him ... if that's the way he wants it," Jerry said rather enigmatically, and a hundred questions rose to plague Karen that she knew she couldn't possibly ask. Not now, not when Michael, in effect, had thrust her out of his life with a firmness that she didn't have the strength to defy.

"It's absolutely beautiful today," Maida said the next morning. "We're going to drive up to Montreal; Jerry and I haven't been there since our honeymoon. There's a little restaurant in the old French quarter we're going to try to find again. Want to come along with us?"

Karen shook her head. "I really should go help the judge today," she said slowly. "It will be my last chance."

Maida stopped short. "What do you mean by that?"

"Maida, I've got to get back to New York," Karen said, the words coming in a faster rush than she had intended. "This isn't fair to Hugh. I've been here ten days already."

Maida's beautiful blue eyes were troubled. "But it would be dreadful to leave now," she began, only to break off as Jerry came into the room. He had just shaved and was smelling of tangy lotion and also looking rested and handsome, as his eyes caressed his wife.

"Who is going to leave?" he demanded.

"Karen," Maida said, her voice close to a wail. "Tell her that she can't, will you?"

Jerry raised his eyebrows, but he merely said, "I

hardly can *tell* her, love. But I *am* surprised, Karen. I suppose I thought you'd become involved to the point where you'd want to . . . see things through."

She smiled sadly. "It isn't a question of what *I* want, Jerry," she told him. "It's simply that I'm not wanted."

"You're sure of that?"

"Well," she said, "he made it abundantly clear, shall we say?"

"He's an idiot!" Jerry exploded shortly.

Maida glanced with some asperity from one to the other of them. "You're talking in riddles, both of you," she complained.

Karen shook her head. "No, we're not really. It's simply that I got into something I shouldn't have gotten into, Maida, and now I think it's better if I get out. In fact, I've been asked to get out."

Jerry's mouth was taut. But he only said, "Then maybe it is for the best. Smarter of you, anyhow."

Her cheeks were burning. "I wasn't thinking of being smart," she said.

Jerry smiled at her, a lopsided smile. "I admit I'm relieved to hear that. Did I tell you Mike and I are going to Nashua together? Maybe tomorrow."

"No."

"You are both driving me absolutely crazy," Maida interjected. "What is all the mystery?"

"I'll fill you in later," he promised. "Now, go get your traveling clothes on, love. I want escargots for lunch."

When Maida had trailed off to their bedroom, Jerry said urgently, "Karen, I know your feelings have been hurt. It sticks out all over you, and I can't blame you. But try not to be too resentful, will you? It isn't that I'm trying to take Mike's part, but he is a rather...special kind of person."

Her voice not nearly as steady as she wanted it to be, she said, "Yes, I've noticed that."

"Also," Jerry continued, his own voice none too steady, "he's been through a hell most of us never even come close to imagining, thank God. And, from his point of view, he's come out of it tarnished."

As Karen looked up in surprise, he added, "That may be a funny way to describe it, but I think it's exactly how he feels about himself. He isn't sorry for himself, I don't mean that. But I think he feels very much apart from the rest of us. Having been in prison *is* a stigma, there's no use trying to deny it. And even if, somehow, Mike's name could be cleared, he's still *been* there, Karen. The sights, the smells, the living, and the pure misery of those three years can't be expunged. I don't mean to say that Mike's entire life is going to be ruined because of those three years. I pray, for that matter, that someday he'll come back into the world, our world. But in the meantime don't be too harsh in your judgment of him."

"I'm not," she said weakly. "The problem is that I can't reach him, Jerry."

"You've come closer to reaching him than anyone else has," Jerry said. "He just doesn't want to admit it, that's all—and especially he doesn't want you to know it. He's a very strong person, Karen. I doubt if I could have even a semblance of his strength under similar conditions. But right now he's carrying a burden that would break most of us." He sighed. "Mike's problem is that he's also carrying a big mental whip, and every time he thinks he's about to step out of line he uses it on himself."

"He uses it on some other people too," Karen said, her lips trembling.

"I know," Jerry agreed. "I've been one of them."

Maida, beautiful in a pale jade slack suit, came out to say, "You two look so grim! Gerald Stanhope, you're going to tell me exactly what this is all about the moment we start out of the driveway!"

"Yes, ma'am!" Gerald Stanhope agreed meekly.

The house seemed so empty after Jerry and Maida left that Karen could not bear staying alone in it, and this was unusual for her. She started out for the judge's house, but this time opted for the easy way and took the path through the woods, circling around Rod's cottage. As she did so, she heard someone shout and saw Rod on the lakefront below, busy with a rowboat that had been freshly painted a bright blue. Everyone seemed to be getting their boats in order just now.

"I'm going to try her out," Rod said. "Got to be sure she's seaworthy. Want to go along?"

"I can't," Karen called back. "I'm working for the judge."

"Lucky man! Hey, are you really going to spend the night on the island with the Barnes kid?"

"What?"

Rod laughed. "The judge was saying last night that Ambrose has taken quite a fancy to you, and he intends to invite you to go on an overnight trip out to the island with him."

"Maybe ten years from now!" She smiled back at him, then waved and continued on her way.

Once at the house, she let the bronze door knocker rise and fall and waited, but there was no answer. The three garage doors were all closed, which could, or could not, mean that everyone had gone out. She hesitated, about to go back to Maida's, then shrank from the thought of being alone again. Nor did she welcome the other alternative, which was spending at least a part of the day in Rod's company. Ebullient though he was, she just wasn't in the mood for him right now.

She remembered that the judge had told her to feel free to go into the house and start work anytime she wanted to, and now she decided that she would do precisely that. If after a time he didn't return, she would write him a farewell note and she almost hoped that this was the way it was going to happen. It would be a lot easier to say good-bye to the judge in writing than face-to-face.

The door was unlocked. Karen walked into the hushed atmosphere of this home that, over the years, had sheltered so much love, and she wished that it had been her personal privilege to have known Eleanor Stanhope.

She moved across the foyer to the living room, her eyes instinctively going to the piano. Briefly she fought an impulse and then yielded to it. She went over and sat down on the bench, her fingers caressing the keyboard.

Then, without even realizing what she was about to do, she found herself plunging into Beethoven, into the sonata *Pathétique,* which precisely matched her mood of the moment, yielding to the sorrow and the passion. Finally she came to the last chord, struck it, and then leaned back, at once spent and amazed.

It was not perfect, of course. It was a long way from perfect. But Michael had been right. It was still there. If she willed it, it would be possible to return to the concert stage, and now she knew it.

"I told you, didn't I?" a quiet voice said.

She swirled around to find Michael standing just behind her. He was wearing the faded jeans and his old green shirt, and his hair was tousled so that despite its pewter color it made him look extremely youthful. He stood with his arms folded, and there was something so vulnerable about his stance that she could feel her resistance begin to melt, even though she had promised herself that she was through with being putty in his hands, subject to his whims.

"Don't you believe in ever announcing your presence?" she said curtly. "Do you always sneak up on people?"

"No," he said levelly, "in answer to both questions. But in this instance you would have stopped playing if you had known I was in the room. And I wanted to hear the *Pathétique*—or the part of it you played—all the way through. It is one of my favorites."

It was one of her favorites too, but she was not about to tell him this. No need to pretend that they had any interests in common, for he would later be the first one to disclaim them.

He came closer, stood over her, and said quietly, "I'm sorry if I startled you. As a matter of fact, I was in the library when I heard you begin to play." His voice deepened. "It was beautiful, Karen, so very beautiful. But there's more to it than the fact of your having made beautiful music, of course. What's important is that it's all there again. You must know that yourself, don't you?''

"No," she disagreed. "It really isn't quite all there again."

"I don't see how you can say that. It seems to me that your nuances of feeling, your interpretation, are even better than they were the last time I heard you. But then of course," he conceded, "I'm not a music critic."

She didn't answer this, because actually she wasn't thinking of music at all. Her mind, her heart, every ounce of her, were filled with this man who stood beside her and she sat as if rooted to the bench, knowing that even were she able to resume her career, as he insisted she could and should do, playing would mean nothing again to her unless he was forever in her audience.

If he could share it all with me, it would be such a different world for both of us. If I could know that he was out there listening, if I could feel his pride in me. And if I knew that later I could go into his arms. . . .

She sat rooted to the piano bench, the knowledge of her overwhelming love for him such a giant thing that she felt small and insignificant in comparison.

How could she keep such knowledge from him? Just now neither of them was ready to handle the scope of such a love, she knew that, and were he to realize the vast extent of her feelings he would be the first to tell her so, the first to rebuff her.

Or would he? What would he do if right now, right this minute . . . ?

She forced her thoughts to trail away from potential peril and became aware that he was looking down at her curiously. "What's the matter?" he asked her, and she knew that warm color was suffusing her face and would be too clear a symptom not to betray her.

"Nothing . . . really," she said tightly.

"I suppose you came to see Dad," he said, and she knew that if he had noticed the flush in her cheeks he evidently was going to disregard it. For that matter, there seemed a new tautness to his voice, and she couldn't bring herself to look at him.

"Dad's gone to visit an old friend of his up in St. Alban's," he explained. "They were going to have lunch together. It's a twice-a-year sort of thing. A couple of old cronies reminiscing, Dad always says."

"I see," Karen said blankly.

"Did Jerry and Maida go to Montreal?" Michael asked, and she had the feeling that he was making conversation to fill in gaps that he didn't dare leave open any more than she did. "They were talking last night about making a day trip up there."

"Yes, they did," she nodded.

"I had the idea that you were going to go along with them."

"They did ask me," she admitted. "It seemed pretty obvious to me though that if they had a choice they'd rather be alone. And I wanted to finish up a few of the things I was doing for your father." She hesitated, and then added with difficulty, "It will be the last chance I have before I leave here."

Inadvertently she glanced up at him just in time to see his jaw tighten, and she would have sworn that he actually winced. But he was quick at recouping, she'd already learned that, and after a second she almost decided that she'd imagined his reaction. *Wishful thinking*, she thought dolefully. *Don't fool yourself into thinking that it means that much to him whether you stay or whether you leave, Karen.*

Silence stretched between them, and she got the impression that, quick camouflage artist though he was when it came to covering up any display of emotion, Michael had been a bit rocked by her announcement.His tone was almost too expressionless as he asked, "Are you going back to New York?"

"Yes," she said.

He hesitated, then to her surprise he asked, "Is it necessary? What I mean to say is, Dad is going to be pretty disappointed. You've really gotten him into this project of his. He'd been talking a lot about it, but frankly he'd been doing very little. He needed an incentive, which you've certainly provided. I know I've no right to suggest that you might consider changing your plans, and I know you do have a job to return to. But if there were any way that you could stick with Dad for just a little while longer, until he has his work really underway...."

Karen couldn't believe her ears. She stared up at him, and then she said, "Am I really hearing you, Michael? It seems to me that I was asked to leave. Rather definitely, I would say."

"Yes," he said gravely. "I know you were. But I was talking to Jerry again—"

"I don't see what Jerry has to do with it," she interrupted. "It was you who made it clear you didn't want me here, and that can't have changed so quickly, can it?"

"I was speaking from a—a personal point of view that isn't easy to explain," Michael said, and she saw to her astonishment that he was actually reaching out for words. "Common sense still tells me that it would be best for you to leave here and get on about your own living. You have a lot of life to live, Karen. Your career again and—"

She flared at this. "Is all you think of in connection with me my musical career?" she demanded. And, without even knowing what she was doing, she stood up to confront him with a belligerence that was very much at variance with her appearance.

Something sparked in his eyes but it was certainly not anger. With a trace of something that she identified as amusement, difficult though that was to believe, he said, "No, I can't say that the only thing I think about in connection with you is your musical career, Karen. Our relationship would be a great deal simpler—and safer—were that the case."

Their eyes meshed, and she caught her breath. Then he said hoarsely, with a hopelessness that tore at her, "Oh, my God, dearest, what in hell am I going to do about you?"

They moved together, as if to fuse by common accord. And this time when their lips met it was in a searing kiss that became a torch, totally incendiary in its impact.

She felt the pressure of Michael's body as he pulled her close to him; she felt the dominating fact of his maleness, and everything in her responded, rising to meet the need that she knew she now shared with him.

His hands were moving downward over her body,

outlining the gentle curve of her hips, and she arched herself even closer, matching urgency with urgency.

And then the phone rang.

It broke the spell. Michael swore audibly but the mood had been shattered. As he left the room to answer this precipitate summons Karen could feel herself sag, the weakness that crept over symbolic of pure frustration.

He was gone only a moment. But when he returned, a tightness had overtaken him. "Would you believe this? That was Ambrose. The kid must be psychic! He's reminded me that I promised I'd teach him how to cast with a fly rod today, and I was supposed to pick him up half an hour ago. Once he's out of school we're planning to head for the mountains on a camping trip, and we want to try to latch on to some trout."

He shook his head ruefully. "Karen, I'm sorry!"

Looking at him, she marveled at the way he always seemed to be able to regain control so quickly. Her attempt to match him was not entirely successful, she knew, but nevertheless she managed to sound fairly crisp about it as she said, "That's all right. Go ahead and get Ambrose. I'm going to finish up the work I'd planned to do for your father, and then I'll get along."

She saw him swallow hard, and knew that he wasn't as calm as he pretended to be after all. He said, "Look, we're going to have to talk about this. About your going away, that is."

"Maybe later," she evaded, and he had to be content with this. But he gave her a long look before he left the room.

"It will only take a few minutes for me to go over and get Ambrose," he told her. "After that, we'll be right down on the lakefront...in case you need anything."

Karen couldn't meet his eyes but she managed to say, "I don't expect to need anything."

A short time later she realized dismally that Michael and Ambrose were indeed down on the lakefront. As she typed she could hardly keep herself from glancing toward the water's edge, where they stood with their long, slender fishing poles. Ambrose was watching Michael with obviously rapt and adoring attention. Watching them, she thought whimsically that she would have never believed she would one day be downright envious of a twelve-year-old boy!

After a time Ambrose came in to say that they were making peanut butter and jelly sandwiches for lunch and to ask if she wanted some. She longed to join them, but she couldn't face being with Michael again, not just now. The mere thought was too nerveracking. She told Ambrose that she was nearly through with her work and thought she'd go ahead and finish and get lunch later, and Ambrose, in typical boy fashion, didn't press the point.

She left her papers stacked neatly for the judge, adding a brief note that she found very hard to write. She thought of telling him that she would stop by the next morning en route to say good-bye, then realized that this would only make it more difficult for both of them.

As she found an envelope in which to put the note, and then wrote the judge's name on the face of it, she felt a sharp pang of loss. She was going to miss him very much.

She promised herself that as soon as possible she

would have the peridot he had given her made into a pendant. She had wrapped it in a handkerchief ever since the day he presented it to her, keeping it in her handbag and taking it with her wherever she went. Now she took it out and stared into its cool pale green depths, as if trying to find comfort in the touch of it.

Always the peridot would remind her of Michael's eyes.

Chapter Thirteen

Michael and Ambrose were back on the lakefront again when Karen left the judge's house, but they seemed to have stopped practicing casting and instead had turned their attention to Michael's boat. She could not tell from this distance just what it was that was engrossing them.

She thought of going down the steps and walking back along the lakefront herself, thus staging a confrontation of sorts, but she decided against it and instead opted for the path through the woods. As she circled around Rod's cottage, she half hoped that he would come out to suggest coffee or a drink. Just now she would have accepted such an invitation, even from June. But no one appeared.

The farmhouse seemed to have acquired new dimensions. Now it wasn't merely "Maida's house," it was very definitely "Jerry and Maida's house," which gave it quite a different significance.

Karen made herself a cup of tea and stood at the window looking out at the lake, watching Michael and Ambrose still working on the boat. She knew that she should call Hugh MacKnight and tell him to expect her back to work the day after tomorrow, but she could not force herself to go to the phone and dial his number. There would be time enough later to do that, and to pack and ready herself for tomorrow's trip. She should, for that matter, check out her airplane reservation from Burlington to New York.

She deplored her own lassitude, because obviously it was vital at this point to get away from Grand Isle, to leave Maida and Jerry to their own renewed happiness, and to put Michael Stanhope behind her—if that were possible.

She frowned. She would never be able to put Michael behind her in the total sense of the word, she realized that only too well. Whether she liked it or not, he would be a part of her for the rest of her life. She was reminded of the words of a Spanish song she'd once known, which, translated, meant that for all the romances in one's life one really loved only once.

Michael would never know it, but he was the one love in her life, and there was no altering this fact. She could never love in this way again.

Nor, she knew now, could she simply go off and set about living her life and resuming her musical career, as he had suggested, while everything concerning Michael and the matter of Chad's death was still so unresolved.

Her trip to Nashua had been a disappointment. She'd not really let herself face just how much of a disappointment, and in a sense, the whole thing had been somewhat overshadowed by the unexpected encounter with Jerry.

Maybe if she could have had more time with Susan Petsky she might have managed to really communi-

cate with the girl, she mused, finishing her tea and
putting down the cup and saucer while she still continued to stare out at the lake.

Michael's back was turned to her, and Ambrose
was deeply engrossed in their common project. She
had the opportunity now to study that silhouette so
beloved to her. The broad shoulders, the tapered
waist, the intensely masculine body. The memory of
that body thrust against her came back to bring an
urgent rush of feeling that she knew she must manage
to suppress if she were going to maintain her sanity.

There were other things to think of now than the
sensual aspects of her feelings toward Michael, she
reminded herself sternly. With an effort she thrust
thoughts and memories aside to concentrate on the
fact that nothing, nothing, could ever really ease the
way for Michael and herself unless—or until—that
cloud hanging over him was dispersed. And she was
convinced that Susan Petsky was the person who held
the key to doing that.

Jerry had said that he and Michael were going to
make a trip to Nashua tomorrow. They would be visiting Susan—at least Jerry would. Karen wondered if
Michael would be willing to confront the girl himself
once the moment was at hand. And perhaps Susan,
secure in her own happiness as a new mother, would
be more willing to explore her memory about that terrible night. No one could blame her for wanting to
forget it forever, but somehow she had to be made
aware of the fact that in a very real way the life of a
man lay in her hands. Michael Stanhope's life.

Karen sighed. It seemed such a blind alley, all of it.
She could understand why Michael must feel that

there could be nothing but a blank wall to bump into at the end of it. Susan was the only hope. But would she talk freely to Jerry or, perhaps especially, after all this time, to Michael?

Karen had the peculiar conviction that if Susan were going to talk to anyone at all—assuming, of course, that she had something to talk about—she would almost surely do so more readily with another woman than she would with a man, to say nothing of two men.

Possibly Maida's help should be enlisted, Karen thought, nearly posing the thought out loud as a question. Then she shook her head. Maida was an expert actress, true, but she couldn't quite see Maida winning Susan Petsky's confidence, whereas she, herself....

This line of reasoning was becoming so obvious that she took her cup and saucer out to the kitchen and nearly slammed it on the counter in her impatience. Then, without stalling any longer, she called the Burlington airport and made a reservation for the first afternoon flight available the next day. This done, she nearly dialed Hugh MacKnight's office, only to remember in time that this was Saturday. Neither Hugh nor Trudy Richardson was usually in the office on Saturday afternoons. She decided to wait and call one or both of them from her apartment tomorrow evening once she was settled in.

She already knew that Brad Simmons was on duty this afternoon. Later, she decided, she'd call the hospital and have him paged so that she could say a brief good-bye. And that, she considered ruefully, would pretty well tie up the ends as far as her Vermont hiatus was concerned.

She shook herself, both physically and mentally, hating self-pity as she always had. An immediate change of scene was needed to chase away the cobwebs, she decided, and purely on impulse she took her purse, car keys, and a sweater, and headed north on Route Two.

She drove the length of Grand Isle and on to North Hero, and then on to the Alburg peninsula, which thrust south from Canada. The scenery was glorious. Karen feasted on tantalizing glimpses of deep blue water, fragrant green pines, and backdrops of towering mountains against a hyacinth-colored sky. And she wished fervently that she had someone beloved to share it all with her.

She stopped for coffee and a hamburger in Alburg Center then went on across the bridge that spanned the northern tip of Lake Champlain, coming to Rouses Point, where, ahead, she saw the Stars and Stripes fluttering on one side of the road, and Canada's stunning red maple leaf flag on the other. Customs. Although she had known, of course, that it was there, it came as a surprise to find that Canada was so close.

It was tempting to continue on, to cross the border and wander aimlessly through some of the little villages in French Quebec, which, she had been told, could be surprisingly European. But her arm had begun to ache, a warning that between piano playing and typing and driving she had given it enough of a workout for one day. So she turned back.

She stopped at the Barneses' general store for a can of beef stew, which would do well enough for a solitary dinner, and she and Roger Barnes passed the time of day without really saying much to each other.

Leaving, she more than half wished that Ambrose would loom up, as he had earlier in the week, but he didn't. Probably, she decided, he was still with Michael.

Back at the farmhouse Karen made herself a drink—something she seldom did when she was alone—then sat down with two magazines she had bought at the General Store. They had some engrossing articles to which she tried to give her attention, but inevitably her mind wandered.

She found herself thinking again of Susan Petsky and was tempted to call the Nashua hospital to ask how she was doing, and, perhaps, whether she'd had a boy or a girl. Then she reminded herself, sternly, that anything concerning Susan was now in Jerry and Michael's hands and absolutely none of her business.

Around eight o'clock Maida phoned to say that she and Jerry had run into some car trouble, which had been diagnosed as a broken water hose. They had been driving down Sherbrooke Street in the middle of Montreal, Maida said, when the engine started to heat up. Fortunately Jerry had been able to find a garage with a mechanic who was willing to work on Saturday night, but he definitely was not noted for his speed. They had decided it would be best to stay over and they would be at the Queen Elizabeth should she need them.

Karen assured Maida that she wouldn't need them, and also promised that she would not leave for the first lap of her trip to New York before they got back in the morning.

She exhausted the magazines and went back to the

mystery novel she had started reading shortly after her arrival on Grand Isle, reading until drowsiness overtook her. Then she fell into a deep and dreamless sleep, only to awaken suddenly for no particular reason at all. After that she found that the harder she tried to get back to sleep the more elusive the task proved to be.

Eventually she got up and made herself a cup of hot milk. She took it over to the living room and stared out through the darkness at the lake. Unfortunately it was cloudy, with no moon to offer silver revelation, and the stars were blotted out.

Karen was about to turn away when she saw something stab through the darkness—a light that flicked on and off, making a pattern.

Someone was out there in the darkness, and they were flashing a signal: three short dots, three long ones, three short ones.

SOS!

The light stabbed the blackness, stopped, then started again, and Karen could feel her pulse begin to race. The light was coming from the island, she was sure of it, and immediately her thoughts turned to Ambrose. The crazy youngster had asked her to go out and camp with him sometime; Rod Kensington had mentioned this only yesterday. She had taken it for granted that Ambrose was thinking a long way ahead, though. Hadn't he even said something about doing this when he was old enough?

No matter. Ambrose, she was certain, was out there, either on the island or on the lake in a boat. Especially if it were the latter, he could be in real trouble!

Her instinct was to seek help. The first thought was of Michael, then she cast away the thought of calling anyone. The vision of Ambrose in a boat that might be sinking and the horror of cold, dark water decided her. Every instant now was wasted precious time that could not be brought back!

Jerry had beached his boat just beyond the water's edge. Karen would not have believed that she could find the strength to shove it into the water, but she did. She threw off her slippers and climbed in, putting the flashlight she had thought to bring beside her. Then she groped for the oars and started rowing. Almost at once, her arm protested with a cramplike spasm of pain, but she kept on going.

It was years since she had rowed and she had never been that good at it, but now everything her father had taught her came back. The idea was to try to keep headed in a straight line, toward the light, which was not as easy as it seemed.

Now her arm really was aching. She gritted her teeth, forcing herself to keep on, her eyes riveted to the stabbing light; then, suddenly, there *was* no more stabbing light.

She held her breath, waiting for the silent plea to begin again, but it didn't. In a moment of total horror she felt water edging around her feet, icy, insidious, invading.

Jerry, she remembered now, had said something about needing to work on the boat, but it had never occurred to her that it would not be watertight. Clearly, though, there was a leak, and she sought desperately to find it.

She groped for the flashlight, turning on the switch

only to find that it cast a pale glow of very little use. It was too small a flashlight with too little power, just as her own power, and that supercharge of strength she had marveled at had evaporated as quickly as it had arisen.

She forced herself to fight panic, forced herself to remember her father and the rudimentary lessons he had given her about boating and about the water. They were lessons that remarkably still stuck with her despite the years of disuse.

It was proving impossible to find the source of the leak, even though now she tried to explore with her fingers. But there was too much water; the level was slowly rising. Still, she reminded herself, the boat would not, should not, sink, and this was what she fought valiantly to remember when every instinct called upon her to plunge into the water and start to swim toward supposed safety. The boat would *float,* even if the top became flush with the water, as indeed it would once it was full.

Yes, it would float, and this meant that she must stay with it. She could remember her father saying that this was the first rule of boating: Always stay with the boat and wait for help to come.

Silently finalizing this sentence, a sob rose in Karen's throat. Help! *What* help?

She couldn't hazard a guess at the water temperature, she only knew that it was very cold. She pulled her feet up, straddling the wooden plank that served as a center seat, and decided to keep out of the water as long as possible, then go over the side and cling to the rim of the boat until daylight. Only then would she be able to gauge whether she was nearer to the lakeshore or to the island and know in which direction to start to swim.

Daylight was still hours away though, and while she couldn't hazard a guess at the water temperature it surely was extremely cold. The water was steadily creeping higher, it was touching her feet. Waves of cold began to seep through her, and she started to shiver violently. Then, because she knew that she should have on as little as possible to avoid being weighted down once she was in the water, she threw off Maida's lavender quilted parka, which she had snatched up at the last instant, said a silent prayer, and slipped over the side of the boat, her legs dangling down into what seemed like ice water. She groped for the edge of the freeboard, but it was wet and clammy to her touch and she felt her fingers slipping on the slick wooden surface. And she knew that, with her right hand at least, she had no strength at all left with which to hold on.

All of the terror in the world seemed to funnel into a single capsule. Karen heard someone screaming and couldn't believe that this was the sound of her own voice.

Somewhere there was a voice. A wonderfully familiar voice. There was strength to the voice; this was what struck at Karen even as she felt herself close to losing consciousness. She tapped this invisible source of strength and mentally clung to it.

"Grab the oar!" the voice called and then repeated more urgently, "Look, Ambrose is holding the flashlight steady on it. Now grab the oar!"

She reached blindly, she touched smooth wood,

she managed to clutch with her good left hand and then she felt the pull, the drag. Michael's arms were lifting her, and she felt as if she were being transported to heaven.

"Mike, she isn't drowned, is she?" she heard Ambrose say.

"Of course not, Ambrose!" Michael snapped and those professional fingers of his actually were fumbling as he stripped off his own jacket and put it around her. Then for a moment he held her so closely to him that she felt her breath would give out.

She felt him shudder, then he said, "Give me back the oar, Ambrose, and just sit still yourself, will you? Karen's going to be all right."

Karen's going to be all right! Those were the last words she remembered. They rang in her ears as Michael started to row strongly, steadily, until, after what seemed an eternity, he said, "It's not much farther." She opened her eyes to look toward the shore, and she saw the silhouette of the big green house ablaze with lights. Looking toward it, Karen decided that it was the most beautiful place in the world, and she began to sob. . . .

After they had reached the shore Michael carried her inside the house, and the judge, propelling his wheelchair across the foyer said, shaken, "Child. Thank God you're safe!"

She wanted to answer him, but Michael didn't stop long enough to let her do so. He carried her directly up a flight of stairs into a large room centered with a big four-poster. She could hear water running somewhere, and she heard Michael say, "That's right. Warm, but not too hot."

Someone else said "Yes," and still in Michael's arms, she looked up to see Horace staring down at her, his big, ugly face creased with anxiety.

"Horace, take Ambrose home, will you," Michael said sternly, "and tell him that once his parents finish with him I'm going to have quite a bit to say to him tomorrow myself!" It seemed to Karen that his grip on her tightened for just a second, and then he said, "I'm going to let you stand up now, but take it easy, do you hear?"

Her feet touched the ground and she tried them out gently. They were numb, they were useless... no, they could hold her up. This she discovered, second by second.

"Now," Michael said, "take your clothes off." And, when she hesitated, "Look, we're alone, and I *am* a doctor. For God's sake, I won't even look at you—not the way I might like to anyway! Just get your clothes off and then get into the bathtub. I'm staying with you. You might pass out."

The sodden clothes dripped in little puddles at her feet. Carefully, for she was still very weak, she got into the tub and sank into blissful warmth. From the doorway Michael asked, "Are you all right?"

She found her voice, but it sounded very small. "Yes."

"You can add a little more hot water from time to time. I want you to get warm all the way through."

She did as she was told, reveling in the deliciousness of not being cold until, much too soon, he said, "That's enough. Now, watch it as you get out. Take it slowly!"

He first handed her an oversize bath towel, then he

was wrapping her in something much bigger. She identified it as a terry robe, which, she was sure, belonged to him, for she could have folded it around herself and still had yards to spare.

He picked her up so quickly that she didn't have time to protest, and carried her effortlessly across to the four-poster, then set her down on the edge of it. He held out a cup of something that smelled like whiskey mixed with spices. "Drink some of this. Slowly."

She did so, and the effect was wonderful. Finally she glanced up at Michael almost timidly and saw a smile twist the corner of his mouth. "Okay," he said. "We don't want to bomb you out before you get settled in! Give me back the robe and the towel and slip into these pajamas. Okay?"

The pajamas were a deep shade of blue, made of the softest flannel she had ever felt and unquestionably they too belonged to him. He laughed once she had put them on, and reached over to roll back the legs and the sleeves. Then he said, "All right. Into bed with you! I've turned on the electric blanket—a little on the high side, perhaps, but I want to get you really warm."

Karen lay back against the pillows and said, actually surprised, "I think I really may feel warm again after all."

Michael smiled at her, and this was a total smile, so devastating that she was afraid she couldn't handle it without becoming swamped by emotion. He reached out and touched her hair and said, forcing lightness, "Pretty damp at the edges, but I'm afraid the establishment doesn't feature a hair dryer."

She tried to smile back but her lips trembled and Michael said hastily, "Don't cry. Please don't cry, Karen. There's nothing to cry about now." Then he added quickly, "Doze off, if you want to. I'm going to get into some dry things myself."

She noted that his shirt was soggy and he said, following her gaze, "You were a pretty wet load. Hey, don't cry!"

Swiftly he bent and kissed her squarely on the lips, and before she could rally he said, "I'll be back in a minute. If you doze off, I'm going to wake you up. You've a bit of explaining to do!"

Karen did doze off, Michael's hot toddy plus the warmth of the blanket proving to be an unbeatable combination. When he first spoke to her again she thought for a moment that she must be dreaming and didn't want to open her eyes for fear that she was. But when he repeated her name she decided to open them after all and she found that he was sitting on the side of the bed.

He had changed into fresh jeans and a pale gray turtleneck and he had made himself a drink, which he now sampled.

"All right," he said then, "suppose you tell me just what you were doing out there in the middle of the lake?"

Her lips trembled. She said, so faintly he had to bend close to hear her, "I was trying to rescue Ambrose."

Michael scowled. "That little wretch!" he exploded. "If Roger doesn't take him over the back of his knee, I'll do it myself first thing in the morning!"

"Then he *was* out on the island?"

"Yes, he was out on the island. He happened to notice that Rod's boat was a nice bright blue, all freshly painted, and he decided to try pioneering the trip, just for the fun of it, since he also knew that Rod and June went across the lake to Plattsburgh this afternoon and won't be back till tomorrow. They have friends over there. And Ambrose only intended to stay long enough to have a picnic supper."

Michael sighed. "I guess I'm not as good an influence on Ambrose as the Barneses seem to think I am! I keep teaching him the value of self-reliance, but I certainly didn't intend to have him try to put it into this kind of practice. The problem was that he got fooling around over on the island and time got away from him. He panicked when he thought about rowing back in the dark and sent that fool SOS. Fortunately Horace saw it from the kitchen window and called me, and I realized right away it was Ambrose and what he was up to. I rowed across to haul him back. Then we heard you scream...."

He stared down at her. He said, "I don't think I'll ever forget seeing you there, in the water...." His voice was husky, his eyes intense. "What made you start out like that?"

"I couldn't sleep," she confessed. "I got a cup of milk, and I was standing at the window when I saw the SOS. I was sure it was Ambrose, and all I could think of was that he was in danger out there."

"And so," he said, "you decided to go to his rescue?"

"Yes."

"And it never occurred to you to make certain that the boat you were about to put forth in was watertight?"

Karen, Jerry hasn't used that old tub for the past three years. He was just beginning to get it into shape and as you found out, almost disastrously, it's full of leaks.

"When I heard the scream," he continued, "I somehow knew it was you." The green eyes darkened. "Oh, my God," he said thickly, "I could have lost you!"

She *had* to reach out to him, to touch him, to try to assuage his anguish, and as she did so he lifted her into his arms, his mouth seeking hers with an urgency that swept them along on a riptide of emotion.

They were finding each other with an intensity that went way beyond them, even making her forget the ordeal she just had been through in the overwhelming sweep of her passion for him. She wanted him so terribly, yet almost transcending her own desire was the frantic yearning of wanting to be wanted *by* him. In another moment she knew that she was, she was indeed. No matter what the past might have held nor what the future might bring, just now in this moment spun out of eternity's web, they were coming together and fusing in a mounting surge of fervor that seemed to make them puppets in fate's hands.

She moaned as she touched him, reveling in every contour of his firm body even while she trembled from his touch upon her, carrying with it, as it did, the ability to arouse her to a peak she never before had even approached. His lips found first one breast and then the other, while she fumbled with the heavy brass buckle that clasped the belt of his jeans, and entirely without conscious volition they were, at once, flesh to flesh, striving for unity in the ultimate sense of the word until the entire world seemed to come to a crescendoing end, only to begin all over again....

At length, spent, he stretched out by her side, and she reached across to find his hand, clasping his fingers in hers. There were tears in her eyes, but above all she didn't want him to talk. There must be nothing said that would mar the miracle that had just occurred between them.

If there must be talk, she told herself, it could come later.

Karen slept, only to awake knowing a strange sense of isolation. Then she realized immediately that this was because Michael had left her.

As she lay alone in the big four-poster, it would have been easy, almost easy, to make herself believe that she had been hallucinating. But she smiled a small and secret smile. About this, at least, she knew better!

She sniffed the pillow by her side and could still smell the pine-wood scent of the shaving lotion he used. Impulsively she took the pillow and hugged it to her as she thought of him. Now more than ever she knew that a way must be found to bring him the peace of mind he needed so desperately.

Everything hinged so much on Susan Petsky, even though it was unrealistic, Karen had to admit, to assume that the girl had lied on the witness stand.

Still, it was the only chance. She frowned. On that trip to the hospital with Susan she'd had an impression of fright on Susan's part, a fright unconnected with the fact that she'd been about to have a baby.

Why fright? Karen asked herself now. Why was Susan afraid if she really had nothing to hide?

With dawn stretching ribbons from the east to tinge the lake with color, Karen sat up in bed to find that she was still weak, even trembling, yet determined.

Michael and Jerry were going to *have* to let her go to Nashua with them today. They were going to have to trust her to be the one to speak to Susan.

It was not easy. Jerry was agreeable to her going along on the trip to New Hampshire, but Michael was adamant that she should not do so. In fact, as she looked at his cold, stern profile across the breakfast table from her at the judge's house it was impossible to believe that only hours ago this stranger had been her lover.

Earlier, Horace had knocked at her door to bring her a set of clothes that Maida had sent over. Now she wore beige slacks, a yellow knitted blouse, and yellow espadrilles. Although it was not the outfit she would have chosen to wear for her visit to Susan Petsky, it would do, she told herself. She had no intention of going back home and changing only to have Michael slip off on his own while she did so.

Jerry, who had walked across for coffee and muffins before they took off, said, "Having Karen go with us makes sense, Mike. I think she definitely would have more rapport with Susan than either of us. In any case, what's the harm in trying?"

"Karen has been through enough," Michael said, tight lipped. "I see no reason at all why she should become involved in this any further. If I had known in the first place that she was going to Nashua, I would have stopped her."

"Exactly how would you have managed to do

that?" Karen asked, piqued. "Look, you two, I *am* here, I'm an adult, I understand English, and I would appreciate it if you'd speak to me directly. Also I'd like to know just how you would have stopped me from going to Nashua."

He shook his head. "It doesn't matter," he said, then added, so ungraciously that it was hard not to be daunted by his attitude, "Very well, then. Come ahead, if you must."

Pride almost made her blurt "Thanks, but I don't go where I'm not wanted." But she stifled pride. There were much more important things at stake just now.

The drive was tense. They stopped briefly for lunch, but Karen could force down only half of her chicken sandwich, resulting in a frown from Michael fiercer than any she'd seen before.

At the hospital, though, it seemed to her that he took on a new kind of aura as he went to speak with a resident on duty in the obstetrical ward, and she was reminded of something she had nearly forgotten. That revealing statement he had made when insisting that she undress before him last night rang in her ears.

"I *am* a doctor," he had told her.

Well, she thought, her throat aching for him as he came back to the lounge where she and Jerry were waiting, he *was* a doctor. He was every inch a doctor.

"Susan's had a baby boy, and she's doing fine. She's receiving visitors and," Michael added reluctantly, "it might be a good idea if you go alone, Karen."

Karen nodded, terrified now that the moment was at hand because so much, so frighteningly much, depended on this interview. The long polished corridor with its gleaming floors seemed endless to her, but then finally she turned into a room with two beds and was thankful that Susan's roommate, at the moment, was somewhere else.

Susan, herself, looked very small and pale. Her dark eyes seemed more enormous than ever, dominating the piquant little face that appeared haunted, rather than joyous, as one might have hoped it would.

She said, her voice pitched low, "Why did you come back here?"

And there was something about her tone that made Karen *know*. Pity merged with exultation as she looked down at the woman, and she realized that she was going to have to be strong about this because it was essential, more vital than she ever could hope to express, that Susan tell the whole story.

Karen leaned close and said, her voice trembling, "Susan, somehow I've got to make you understand. No one is going to hurt you. You have nothing to fear. We'll protect you, I promise you that. But Michael Stanhope might as well stay in prison the rest of his life unless you tell me what you know. Otherwise, he will never be free."

She could see Susan's mouth tremble and she said, her own voice so choked that she could hardly force out the words, "Do you want to tell me, Susan?"

"Oh, my God!" Susan Petsky moaned and stared up at her, the huge eyes filling with tears. "Yes, I do. Oh, yes." Then she began to cry.

Chapter Fourteen

They sat in the same diner where she and Jerry had sat only four days before. Michael, glancing across at her, said, "You look terrible. Are you sure you're all right?"

"Yes," Karen said, but she was not all right. She was not all right at all. She yearned to reach out to Michael, to touch him. His face was haggard, emphasizing the grayness of his hair, and his green eyes were bleak as a winter lake. She said, aching for him, "This has been so dreadful for you...."

He shrugged off her pity and said tersely, "It hasn't been exactly easy for Jerry, either."

"It hasn't been easy for any of us," Jerry said gently, including Karen.

Jerry, at the hospital, had become a lawyer rather than a bereaved brother, wrapping himself in a cloak of objectivity, and Karen had admired him tremendously. It was he who had insisted upon taking down Susan's statement and having it witnessed by two of the doctors on the floor.

Now, in the restaurant, he said he felt Susan deserved to be prosecuted for perjury, but Michael shook his head.

Jerry's voice was bitter. "After all, it is because of her that you spent three years in prison," he pointed out.

Michael's face was pure stone and his voice matched it as he said, "There's no need of going into that." His tone left little doubt that this was a door he firmly intended to keep closed.

Karen couldn't repress the words. "Michael, sometime you're going to have to talk about it—"

She couldn't finish. She was beginning to feel more than faintly sick and Michael said sharply, "Karen!" and then added furiously, "Dammit, Jerry, she should be home in bed!"

"No, I shouldn't be!" She looked at him directly, defiantly, and their eyes locked. "I should be exactly where I am!"

Jerry smiled, a weary smile. "She's quite a girl, Mike!" Then, before Michael could comment, he added, "Susan's statement clarifies things, of course. Maybe she'll be able to tell us even more once she calms down. There are still so many gaps."

Yes, Karen thought wryly, Susan's statement had clarified things. But, in a sense, it had made everything almost worse. Now they knew that Susan hadn't even been in the apartment when Chad Stanhope had been killed. She had been with Rod Kensington in a motel several blocks away.

Susan, forcing out the words between sobs, had told Karen that the afternoon of the party a favorite patient of hers had died, a young woman, not much older than she was, who had been an amazingly brave person. The death had depressed her, and when some of the other nurses had suggested she go to a party with them she had been more than glad to accept, even though she seldom socialized very much at the hospital. She was engaged to Walter Petsky, who had been her high school sweetheart and was still in Nashua, and Walter was an extremely jealous man. She knew this, but she loved him and had no desire at all to "stir him up."

That night, though, she drank too much, she met Rod, and there was a quick attraction between the two of them. She found herself telling Rod about the afternoon's tragedy, and he was sympathetic. When the other nurses left the party, Rod urged her to stay on, promising to see her home himself, and she did so. Finally there were just five of them left—Michael, who, she remembered, seemed to be half asleep in an armchair, June Kensington, Rod Kensington, Chad, and herself.

When Rod suggested that the two of them go for a walk to get some fresh air, she had thought it a good idea. When he led her toward the nearby motor inn where he and his sister were staying, she protested only mildly. Rod had a way about him, she admitted to Karen.

They were in Rod's bedroom when the phone started ringing. She remembered that he was swearing as he answered it, and she started laughing at him. Then he turned to her, and there was a terrible expression on his face. He told her only that they had to go back to Chad's right away, but he didn't tell her why.

At the apartment they found June in a state of near

hysteria. Michael, dazed, was leaning over Chad, who was prone on the floor. June kept insisting that Rod try to wake Chad, and when Rod told her that Chad was dead she started crying hysterically and wouldn't believe it.

Finally June said that she and Michael and Chad had been having a final nightcap that had culminated in a crazy kind of argument between the two young men. Chad had gotten out the gun they used to use for target shooting. The next thing she knew, June said, the gun had gone off and then Michael was just standing there and Chad had slumped to the floor.

They'd had a hard time getting even that much out of June in the state she was in, and in retrospect it seemed to Susan that Rod had been the only one capable of thinking clearly. He had told her that she must call the police and when they came she must simply tell them that Chad and Michael had been fooling with the gun, in the course of which it had gone off. This, Rod had said, was after all the truth.

When she had protested, Rod had told her tersely that there was no way *she* could get involved in Chad's death, but it would be a front-page scandal if it became known that he and June, both cousins, had been in the apartment at the time. He made a bargain with her. If she told the police the story he would outline she would be home free, and he and June would be out of it. Otherwise, he promised her, he would have no qualms about describing their earlier rendezvous in his bedroom to her fiancé.

Susan, terrified, had been more in awe of the thought of Walter's wrath than anything else, and it was this that had led her on through the trial, testifying as she had. She knew that Michael was the son of a prominent judge, and she felt certain that people like that would have some influence. Further, he had been "doped up," something had been wrong with him. Anyhow, he had been out of it throughout all the time he'd been at the party, as she remembered it. She was convinced that the whole shooting incident had been some kind of freak accident, and it had never occurred to her that Michael would be convicted.

She had been haunted by a nightmare of pure horror ever since.

Karen was so lost in her reverie that she was aware only of Jerry and Michael talking together in low tones, and she looked up to find Michael's eyes intent upon her face.

"We've got to get you home," he said.

But she shook her head. "Not till we've said what I think has to be said. It must have been June."

Michael stared at her, pure amazement on his face. She flinched, because this only confirmed the feelings she'd had from the very beginning about the importance of the role June had played in his life and would like to play again.

"What could possibly give you such a ridiculous idea?" he demanded, his anger cold.

"I'm not saying that it wasn't an accident," Karen said, wondering if she could find enough strength to keep at this.

"I wouldn't call it an accident at all," Michael told her flatly. "I think Susan's statement makes it pretty clear they convicted the right person!"

He closed his eyes, and Karen saw that Jerry was looking at him anxiously.

Jerry said, his own voice tense, "There's no point in going into it just now, Mike, and he's right, Karen. We've got to get you home. I'd say you've just about had it!"

The drive back across Interstate 89 to Burlington and then on to Grand Isle seemed eternal. Jerry and Michael were both quiet, deeply preoccupied. Karen, exhausted, finally fell into a restless sleep.

It was late afternoon when they reached the farmhouse. Charcoal clouds patterned the gray sky and rain threatened. Maida, coming to the kitchen door, said, "Michael, your father is over here."

A look akin to desperation swept across Michael's face. "Jerry, bring Dad and Maida up to date, will you? I've got to walk a while before I can face them."

Karen, her voice very small, found the courage to ask, "May I come with you?"

He looked down at her as if he had never so much as noticed her before and said curtly, "If you feel you must."

She glanced at Jerry, and saw him nod ever so slightly. But for this she would have faltered. As it was, she said, "Yes, I do feel I must."

Michael did not head for the lakefront this time. Instead he struck out across the fields on the far side of the farmhouse. The ground was rough, and although Karen was wearing flat espadrilles she found it hard going. She stumbled and nearly fell twice, and then finally Michael took her arm and said, with surprising gentleness, "You shouldn't have come. You're exhausted. I'm going to take you back."

"No," she said quickly, urgently, "not yet!"

There was a rawness to the air and she shivered as she spoke. He frowned. "You're cold too. Next thing you know, you'll be down with pneumonia! Come on, we're going back."

She shook her head stubbornly, and even though she was fully aware of his irritation she reached out and touched his sleeve tentatively. "Please!"

"Please, what?"

She swallowed hard. "Please," she said, "don't shut me out."

The silence became crystal between them. Karen looked up into a face no longer carved from stone, she saw his mouth twist with the hurt of pure bitterness and he said, "It's hardly a question of shutting you out, Karen."

"But it is!" she protested impatiently. "All along, you've felt as if you had to face everything, the whole world, all by yourself. I know how you've felt. I've had my own problems and I've felt much the same way. But it—it's not a valid way to be, Michael. Not when people care for you. Anyway, how do you think *I* feel? If I hadn't poked in where you didn't want me to poke, Susan wouldn't have *made* her damned statement."

He smiled very briefly, a smile etched with sadness. "Back when I was studying chemistry, I think we would have called you a catalyst. You have the effect of a catalytic agent, you make things happen while remaining unto yourself, don't you, Karen? But in this case, you're what I'd call a captive catalyst.

You've gotten yourself into a situation you can't get out of."

"Doesn't it occur to you," she asked him steadily, "that I haven't been *trying* to get out of it? Can't you realize—"

He frowned. "You have a very annoying habit of leaving your sentences unfinished," he told her.

"*I* have an annoying habit?" she challenged him. "You never half *begin* your sentences."

"I think I mentioned that I got out of the habit of making polite conversation in prison," he said icily.

She stared up at him, wanting at once to throttle him and to make love to him as they had last night. *Oh, dear God,* she thought, *if only last night could be repeated!* For an instant it seemed to her he was going to take her into his arms and she moved closer to him. But instead he stepped back.

"History isn't going to repeat itself!" he said warningly. "What can I say to you about my behavior yesterday? I was frantic with worry about you, I think once again in my life a drink must have gone to my head. I had no right whatsoever to—to take you as I did."

Was it regret in his voice? He sounded as if he felt he had played the part of traitor—and to whom, she asked herself, achingly, and did not have to be told the answer.

June Kensington. June Kensington, with the deep gold hair and the flashing eyes and that provocative figure that she clothed so cleverly in a whirling mass of colors that would have clashed on anyone else, but looked so right on her.

A whirling mass of colors.

She stared at Michael, her eyes wide, and he asked, swiftly, "What is it?"

"Nothing," she said, and then added, before he could question her further, "Let's get back to the house."

They found Maida and Jerry and the judge in the living room. The judge looked across at Michael quickly, anxiously, and then, somewhat to Karen's surprise, seemed to relax.

"Play bartender for us, will you, Jerry?" he said. "Mike, we've been talking this over. We're going to have to face both Rod and June with this girl Susan's statement."

Michael looked down at his father, pain in his eyes. "Don't all of you realize," he asked softly, "that it's too late? I've served my sentence and Chad is dead. Nothing any of us can do will bring him back!"

"There is such a thing as justice, Michael," the judge said.

"So there is," Michael said levelly. "And who am I to say whether or not it misfired when I can't even remember what happened?"

"June can remember," Jerry said softly, "if we are to believe Susan Petsky."

"*Can* we believe Susan Petsky?" Michael countered.

He's protecting June, Karen thought, and the knowledge made her feel ill. *Even when he knows what she did to him, he's still protecting her!*

Michael sighed deeply. He said, his voice heavy, "I'm as glad Rod and June are still over in New York

State, just now. Jerry, make me another drink, will you?''

Karen had never seen his eyes look so dark, and watching him, she realized that this was how he would look when he was years older, as old as the judge was now.

"The reason I wanted to go to Nashua with you, Jerry," Michael began, "was because I wanted to tell Susan not to change her story. It was impossible to do that, though, because Karen had gotten into the picture and I knew only too well she wouldn't stop until she'd talked to Susan herself. I also knew that Susan had the need we all have to confess... when the chips are down.

"You see," he continued, accepting the glass that Jerry now handed him, "if anything at all, Chad killed himself."

Jerry's quickly indrawn breath was clearly audible, and Michael added hastily, "Not deliberately. Certainly not deliberately. That night, the night of the party... well, the whole thing was a kind of terrible game. Chad wanted to get me high. He and June thought it would be funny, because I'd been working so damned hard I had no time to party with them. They spiked my coffee, but I think they didn't consider the effect of caffeine. Evidently the stuff they used, in combination with caffeine, created the effect of a downer, rather than an upper. Combined with the couple of drinks I'd had, it put me out of the picture. I didn't come to until it was... all over. At least I don't remember what I did or said.

"Somehow, though, I did remember a whirl of color, and later I made the association with the dress

June was wearing that night. Much later, I might add. We all know that June's always gone in for crazy color schemes, but at the time I was arrested I thought the colors were just part of some overall hallucination.

"When I got out of prison, though, I went to see June down in Texas, just as I came to see you, Jerry. By then, I had a very strong feeling that she had been in the room when Chad died. Well," Michael said, and took a long draft of his drink, "as people do, she too wanted to unburden herself. She told me that after Rod and Susan went off that night, Chad began to get pretty ugly about things. Chad accused June of having an affair with me."

"Do you blame him?" Jerry said tightly. "I think June has always been in love with you."

Michael shook his head. "On the contrary, June was always in love with Chad, ever since they both were kids, and he returned it. They were first cousins by blood, though, but Chad had already told me that eventually they were going to marry anyway. They simply had made a pact they would never have kids, as a precautionary measure.

"Anyway, for some reason Chad got jealous that night. He started taunting me, but I was too out of it to do much more than respond in monosyllables and this only made him madder. Finally he got out that gun we'd so often used for target practice, and I guess he flung a few insults, plus questions, at me. God knows what I answered. Maybe he asked me if I loved June, and I said yes. Maybe he even asked if we'd had an affair and I mumbled yes. Anyway it was something like that, something I didn't even know I was saying, and this infuriated Chad. You've got to remember he'd had a lot to drink, he wasn't himself. He started to threaten me with the gun and June got scared and went to him and tried to get it away from him, and it went off.''

Michael shuddered. ''That's when I began to come to. June was screaming; she was hysterical. She called Rod and he came back with Susan. She's Rod's twin, and twins have a strange kind of closeness sometimes. All Rod could think of was keeping June out of trouble, and all June could think of was the fact that Chad was dead. In some crazy twisted way she really did blame me for it, and Rod believed everything she told him. Much later, after I was in prison, June got to the point where she couldn't live with herself, with her memories, and she went to a psychiatrist who was able to make her finally face the reality of what had happened. But as I've already said, it was too late, and it's too late to do anything now.''

He looked across at Jerry and he said, ''I would say that I have the most right of anyone living to make a decision about this. And I say to leave it alone.''

Jerry sighed. He leaned back, emotionally spent, and Maida took his hand and held it in hers as if he were a small boy.

The judge said slowly, ''I doubt a court in the land would find June guilty of anything—except possibly trying to save your life, Michael. To publicize Susan Petsky's statement would very possibly ruin her marriage; she's told you of her husband's jealousy. Nothing, God knows, can atone for the three years you've spent in hell, but I think it would be even more painful for you if this were dragged through the press again. It seems to me, however, that the most important thing is that you be vindicated."

Wearily Michael said, "June has given me a sworn statement as to the events of that night. It exonerates me, but no, I don't want it to be made public. It will be given to the right people in medicine. I will be able to get my license back and to get back into my own field, where I belong. That's all I ask."

Chapter Fifteen

Karen slept a sleep of pure exhaustion that night. A sleep completely without dreams. She awoke to the realization that it was days since she'd had the nightmare, nor had Saturday night's rowing episode caused a setback with her arm. Her arm, in fact, felt stronger than it had since the accident, with only an occasional, fleeting pain as a reminder.

Hugh's prescription had worked. But the medicine had proved much, much stronger than she had anticipated.

She wandered out to the kitchen and found a note from Maida on the table. Maida had written: "Jerry and I have gone over to Burlington to do some shopping. Be back by midafternoon."

Should she wait until they returned, she wondered, or should she pack and leave while they were still away? She had, after all, played her part. Michael had called her a catalyst, a captive catalyst, at that. Well, catalysts were supposed to be unchanged by the changes they inflicted on others, and they were never able to be captured.

What a myth, what an absolute myth, that was!

This was another magnificent, freshly washed day. It was getting warmer. Maida had opened the side window in the living room, and there was a new summer softness to the air.

Karen heard someone laugh, and she looked out to see Michael and Ambrose down on the lakeshore. They were practicing casting again, and at first she was surprised. This was Monday. Ambrose should be in school, she told herself, and then remembered that the previous Friday had been the last day of school. Now, vacation time stretched ahead. A summer, when there would be camping trips in the mountains for Michael and Ambrose, picnics out on the island, lazy days swimming in the lake or sunning along the shore or out on the flat rocks.

Her eyes stung. Slowly, almost grimly, she went back into her room and dressed in the beige slack suit she had worn up from New York. She made up a bit more carefully than usual, indulged in her favorite perfume, and fastened small gold loops to her ears. Then she left by the kitchen door so that she would not be seen from the lakefront, walking up the road to the fork and down again to the judge's house.

The judge was in his workroom. He seemed tired and very much alone but he looked up with a smile when he saw her. Then he noticed the way she was dressed, and the smile faded.

"You really are going back to New York?" he asked soberly.

She faced him squarely, her chin held high. "To be perfectly honest about it, I'm not sure."

The judge frowned. "I have the feeling you're asking for advice, my dear."

Karen's smile was rueful. "I am, your honor," she admitted.

"Then," the judge said gravely, "I think it becomes a matter of whether or not—in a certain situation—you plead guilty or not guilty."

Karen's smile was tremulous. "I plead guilty. I love him very much."

For a moment the judge actually seemed to sag. Then he recovered and straightened. "Whew! You shouldn't frighten an old man like that!"

"You are *not* an old man," Karen said sternly. "In fact, you're a long way from being old. I'd like to think that you have many years ahead, and that despite everything that's happened they can be wonderful years for you. In fact, I'd even like to think that I might be able to do my bit toward helping in that direction. But whether I can or not, I'm afraid it isn't really going to be up to you or to me, at least to begin with."

"Karen, he's been carrying a terrible burden for a long time. It isn't something he can throw away all at once. Even though he's suspected for quite a while that he didn't pull the trigger that killed Chad, I think he still feels a responsibility for his death. Sometimes trivial things can make vast differences. If Michael hadn't asked for coffee, for instance, would this have ever happened? Those, I imagine, are just a few of the things that still plague him. The fact that they can't be altered, nor that we can never truly know all the answers, can't be changed.

"Also," he said, his voice grave, "neither you nor I, my dear, can ever hope to entirely blot out the stain that prison has left upon him, as I've already told you.

Knowing what I know of prisons, I marvel sometimes that Michael came through as well as he did. Now... well, he's going to have a great deal of adjusting to do, and then a future to plan for."

She thought of June Kensington. Was June included in that future?

"There is something else," the judge said, cutting across her own reflections. "You have your own talent, Karen. You still haven't played for me, though I hope that sometime you will. But Michael tells me that it is still 'all there,' as he puts it."

Karen said, very carefully, "I think it is. But I'm not sure I want it to be, though that may sound insane to you. At least I'm not sure I want it to be the way it was before. I don't say that I never want to play another concert, but I do say that I know now I never want my career to own me again. There are other things...."

"Are you sure," the judge asked her, "that he could be a part of your career...and of those 'other things'?"

She looked down at him. She said, not caring that she was putting her heart in her eyes in front of this man whom she had already come to revere, "He could be all of them. I think the important question is whether or not I could be a part of — of everything to him."

"Speaking as someone who has, perhaps, passed judgment more than he might have wished to, I want to caution you not to leap to conclusions nor to make assumptions that may not be valid. I think he has the right to be heard, Karen," the judge counseled.

Karen frowned. "Does he *want* to be heard? I

think...well, I think if anything is ever going to be *right* between us, he has to make the first move."

"Are you sure about that? Might there not be a question of meeting halfway?"

She looked down at him, then impulsively bent and kissed his cheek. And it was the judge now who looked out the window onto the lakefront below, and who was still watching as Karen left the house and crossed the lawn, and stood at the top of the steps.

Ambrose saw her first. He called out, "Hey, Karen, come on down!" and she made her way carefully down the steps because she was wearing heels today.

Michael straightened, watching her, and then she saw that he was noticing the way she was dressed, and his eyes became like daylight turned to dusk.

"You look as if you're going somewhere," he said.

She nodded, trying to swallow down the knot in her throat. "I'm going to get an afternoon flight back to New York from Burlington," she said. "I have to turn the car in first, though, so I thought I'd leave a bit on the early side."

"Possibly because you can't wait to get away?" he asked, his voice taut.

Ambrose was scowling. "Why can't you stay here?" he demanded directly.

Karen could feel herself flushing, and without wanting to at all, she found herself looking directly into Michael's eyes.

"Yes," he asked, a cool edge to his voice, "why can't you?"

His coolness infuriated her. Trying to keep a grip on herself, she said, "I think you know the answer to that."

"Do I?"

"Please, Michael!"

"Look," Ambrose said, "Mike's right. Didn't you like going fishing out on the island with us?"

"Of course, Ambrose," she said, trying to quell emotions she had no desire to drag out into the open just now. "I loved going fishing with you. But—"

Michael was staring down at her, and she couldn't interpret the expression on his face. Then he said, "Ambrose, Horace was baking something before that smelled pretty good. How about getting lost for a while while you find out what it was? I'd like to talk to Karen alone."

To Karen's surprise, Ambrose grinned, a wide grin that seemed to make every freckle on his face stand out in broad relief. He actually giggled before he turned and scampered up the steps, and it was all Karen could do not to yield to the impulse to call him back.

She had already known that Michael Stanhope could be a formidable man when he wanted to be, but she had never felt quite so small before him as she did now. He said, actually being stern about it, "Did you really think I could let you go so easily?"

"I suppose," she said, "that I didn't think it very much mattered to you. You already made it plain at Maida's last night that I've only...interfered in your life. You came right out and as much as said you wished I'd never spoken to Susan Petsky."

"That was not for my sake, can't you understand that?" he told her. "I saw no reason to—to bring it all out again. But now that it's happened I'm glad it did. I see no point in confronting June with it, that's all."

"You would do almost anything to protect her, wouldn't you?" Karen challenged.

"And just what do you mean by that?"

"Oh, it's so obvious." She had never before felt so weary, so hopeless.

But Michael wasn't about to let it go at that. "Perhaps I'm being unduly dense," he said, "but I don't see that anything is obvious in our situation, Karen. I've fought my feelings for you all the way—except when I literally couldn't help myself—you know that. Now, as a matter of fact, I'm so damned confused about us that I've given up even trying to be logical! Logic tells me I should *let* you walk off and go back to New York because I've no right at all to ask you to share *my* life. We've been through that before."

She was staring at him. "I don't think we have," she corrected. "I don't think you've ever indicated that you would *want* me to share your life, or any part of it. Are you suggesting that I might, after all, have the chance to come in second best to June?"

His eyes flared, and for a moment he looked so angry that she flinched. Then he said, "I'm not sure what you mean."

"Simply, that June loved your cousin Chad, but you've always loved June, haven't you? And now... well, maybe now you'll have a chance with her."

"June is going to marry the man in Plattsburgh whose family she and Rod went to visit last weekend. Their engagement was announced at a party there Saturday night. And, before you start getting the feeling that I'm suffering from a broken heart, let me tell you that June has never had any place in my life other than that of a cousin—by adoption, to be sure. Nevertheless I spent summers and grew up with Jerry, June and Rod, and Chad, remember? Need I elaborate?"

"No," she said, her voice small.

"As for *you*," he continued, "you jolted me out of my senses the first time I saw you."

"And slammed the door in my face?" she reminded him.

"Yes, and slammed the door in your face. But"— he shook his head—"perhaps it would be better to say good-bye now after all."

"Why?"

"Why?" he echoed. His smile was wry. "I have a lot of pieces to pick up and a long way to go before I can even get started again, Karen."

"And you think I haven't?"

"Not in the same way. You've pretty well put your pieces together, though I don't think you fully realize it yet. You've a whole wonderful future waiting for you."

She saw the wistful expression in his eyes, and she knew that sometimes halfway wasn't really enough.

"I have no future at all," she said steadily, taking the final plunge, "unless you're going to be a part of it." She stood tall, her shoulders squared, letting everything she felt for him surface in her revealing face.

"I—I've never been casual about my relationship with a man," she said. "I've never been emancipated enough, if that's the way you want to put it, to take sex lightly. And the other afternoon...I think we both knew that it went far beyond sex, or the impulse of the moment between two adults, Michael. I—I don't know about you, but it's not something I either can forget nor do I want to forget it. But even if it weren't for that, I think I fell in love with you the moment you slammed that door in my face. And ever since—"

His eyes were upon her; he looked at her as if he were in the throes of a vision. He said disbelievingly, "And ever since...?"

Once again Karen could feel herself coming to the end of an emotional rope, which, at best, was very frayed. A moment ago Michael had asked her if she'd really thought he would let her go so easily, but now she wondered if he would have made any real effort to stop her.

She wished that she could have a telepathic communication with the judge because it didn't seem to her that she was getting very far just now. She had "declared herself"—she smiled inwardly at this use of such an old-fashioned term—and yet he was still looking at her skeptically, and she was beginning to realize that a shell she thought had been fragmented might, in fact, still be very much intact.

Trying to smile brightly, she said, "I guess it doesn't make sense, does it? I guess people don't go around falling in love with people who slam doors in their faces."

"Karen," he began, but she only shook her head, feeling as if some sort of tap had been turned on inside her so that she had to keep talking, keep chattering.

"I shouldn't have come down here," she said. "I

should have let you and Ambrose go on with whatever you were doing. It seems as if I'm always interrupting you or probing or prying where I shouldn't pry, and I—"

"You are also babbling," he pointed out to her. Then his tone gentled. "Karen, don't you see? You've no idea what sharing my life would be like!"

She took another plunge. "You don't think I'm cut out to be a doctor's wife, is that it?"

"Don't be ridiculous!" he told her. "Any man in the world—any doctor in the world—would be so lucky to have you for a wife that—"

He paused, and she could see that he was making an almost visible attempt to get control of himself. Camouflage wasn't coming quite so easily at the moment, she realized, and a stab of triumph shot through her.

"I didn't want you to go," he said, "not now, anyway, because I wanted to—to sit down with you someplace where we could be by ourselves and talk things out. There is so much that you need to understand. If they'll have me, I'm going to go back and finish my residency and take it from there. But there's no chance that I'll be able to do anything like that without the media getting wind of it, Karen. The papers will almost surely have their field day. I'll be front-page news again."

"I think the very fact that you'll be allowed back into medicine will be a kind of vindication, Michael."

"Perhaps, in a way. Because there was always a certain element of . . . doubt. About my guilt, that is. But it isn't easy to be exposed publicly, Karen. It tears you up. I couldn't stand to have you face that."

"I've been exposed publicly, though in a different way of course," she reminded him. "Nevertheless, there were a lot of front-page stories... after the plane crash. All the dramatic bits about a young artist injuring her arm. An ultimate cliché that turned into heart-wrenching copy. So I've run the gamut myself, and I know exactly what you mean. But I think you're overestimating all of that, and even if you aren't, it doesn't matter to me. If I didn't have the courage to stand by you through an ordeal that can't possibly last very long—there is too much news to think that they're going to feature you forever—then surely I wouldn't qualify to be—"

She broke off at this, and he asked curiously, "To be what?"

She hesitated for a long moment. Then she gathered up all the inner strength she possessed to say, "To be your wife."

Karen couldn't look at him of her own volition. But after a moment that strong hand she loved so much came to tilt her chin up so that he forced her to meet his eyes. And she saw that there was humor in his smile as he asked, "Am I correct in getting the impression that you're proposing to me, Karen?"

"I..." she began and heard him chuckle.

"When we're both very old and have been married for years and years and years," he told her, "I may remind you of this. But if the facts are really to be known, I've proposed to you a thousand times... in my mind and in my heart. I just never thought I'd find a way to say the words out loud."

There was no camouflage now, no shell. He asked simply, "Will you marry me, Karen?"

And as he drew her into his arms it seemed to her that finally the sorrow that had etched his face for so long lifted, like a cloud being blown away.

She smiled up at him, her adoration evident. "Must you ask the question?"

"Not when I can get the answer in a much better way," he told her, bending his head so that his lips were poised above her mouth. And he proceeded to prove his point.

HARLEQUIN
PREMIERE AUTHOR EDITIONS

6 top Harlequin authors—6 of their best books!

1. JANET DAILEY Giant of Mesabi
2. CHARLOTTE LAMB Dark Master
3. ROBERTA LEIGH Heart of the Lion
4. ANNE MATHER Legacy of the Past
5. ANNE WEALE Stowaway
6. VIOLET WINSPEAR The Burning Sands

Harlequin is proud to offer these 6 exciting romance novels by
6 of our most popular authors. In brand-new beautifully
designed covers, each Harlequin Premiere Author Edition
is a bestselling love story—a contemporary, compelling and
passionate read to remember!

Available wherever paperback books are sold, *or* through
Harlequin Reader Service. Simply complete and mail the coupon below.

- -

Harlequin Reader Service

In the U.S.
P.O. Box 52040
Phoenix, Ariz., 85072-9988

In Canada
649 Ontario Street
Stratford, Ontario N5A 6W2

Please send me the following editions of **Harlequin Premiere Author Editions**.
I am enclosing my check or money order for $1.95 for each copy ordered,
plus 75¢ to cover postage and handling.

☐ 1   ☐ 2   ☐ 3   ☐ 4   ☐ 5   ☐ 6

Number of books checked_____ @ $1.95 each = $ _____

N.Y. state and Ariz. residents add appropriate sales tax $ _____

Postage and handling $ _____ .75

I enclose $_____   TOTAL $ _____

(Please send check or money order. We cannot be responsible for cash sent
through the mail.) Price subject to change without notice.

NAME_____
(Please Print)
ADDRESS_____ APT. NO._____

CITY_____

STATE/PROV._____ ZIP/POSTAL CODE_____

PA–W

Offer expires April 30, 1984.   31056000000

Share the joys and sorrows of real-life love with
Harlequin American Romance!™

GET THIS BOOK
FREE as your introduction to
Harlequin American Romance —
an exciting series of romance
novels written especially for
the American woman of today.

Mail to:
Harlequin Reader Service

In the U.S.
2504 West Southern Avenue
Tempe, AZ 85282

In Canada
649 Ontario Street
Stratford, Ontario N5A 6W2

YES! I want to be one of the first to discover
Harlequin American Romance. Send me FREE and without
obligation *Twice in a Lifetime.* If you do not hear from me after I
have examined my FREE book, please send me the 4 new
Harlequin American Romances each month as soon as they
come off the presses. I understand that I will be billed only $2.25
for each book (total $9.00). There are no shipping or handling
charges. There is no minimum number of books that I have to
purchase. In fact, I may cancel this arrangement at any time.
Twice in a Lifetime is mine to keep as a FREE gift, even if I do not
buy any additional books.

Name _____ (please print)

Address _____ Apt. no.

City _____ State/Prov. _____ Zip/Postal Code

Signature (If under 18, parent or guardian must sign.)

This offer is limited to one order per household and not valid to current Harlequin
American Romance subscribers. We reserve the right to exercise discretion in
granting membership. If price changes are necessary, you will be notified.
Offer expires April 30, 1984

AR-SUB-100

154-BPA-NAFG

Yours FREE, with a home subscription to SUPERROMANCE™

Now you never have to miss reading the newest SUPERROMANCES... because they'll be delivered right to your door.

Start with your **FREE** LOVE BEYOND DESIRE. You'll be enthralled by this powerful love story...from the moment Robin meets the dark, handsome Carlos and finds herself involved in the jealousies, bitterness and secret passions of the Lopez family. Where her own forbidden love threatens to shatter her life.

Your **FREE** LOVE BEYOND DESIRE is only the beginning. A subscription to SUPERROMANCE lets you look forward to a long love affair. Month after month, you'll receive four love stories of heroic dimension. Novels that will involve you in spellbinding intrigue, forbidden love and fiery passions.

You'll begin this series of sensuous, exciting contemporary novels...written by some of the top romance novelists of the day...with four every month.

And this big value...each novel, almost 400 pages of compelling reading...is yours for only $2.50 a book. Hours of entertainment every month for so little. Far less than a first-run movie or pay-TV. Newly published novels, with beautifully illustrated covers, filled with page after page of delicious escape into a world of romantic love...delivered right to your home.